Rare Gems

Holly Schindler

Experience the magic of the original
Ruby's Place Christmas Collection:

Christmas at Ruby's
I Remember You
Sentimental Journey
The Gift That Is Ruby's Place

Ruby's Regulars is the spinoff Ruby's Place series:

Ruby's Story
Rare Gems

Ruby's Place

This Christmas season, as you curl up under your favorite blanket near the warmth of the fire—as you sit near your tree (branches nearly drooping beneath the weight of so many ornaments)—and begin reading this story, the Open sign is being turned to face the sidewalk at Ruby's Place. The red neon sign is popping to life, buzzing against the night sky. Cars are edging their snow-packed tires into nearby parking spaces. The bright green door is swinging as revelers race in, their steps bouncing. Of course, Ruby doesn't run the place, not now. It's been far too many years, and Ruby is herself a memory.

But memories hold a kind of special power inside Ruby's Place. They breathe. They're never out of reach.

Yes, Ruby's Place is open. This Christmas Eve, as you're sitting down to your supper—as the smells of roast turkey and pumpkin pie and dinner rolls fill your kitchen—you'll think of it: the quaint little supper club right there in the midst of the small-town bustle of Sullivan, Missouri. No matter how full your table is, you'll wonder who's there, inside Ruby's. You'll wonder what songs are being sung at the piano, and you'll think of the signature marshmallows and hot cocoa (a special recipe made with real chocolate) that are always served on Christmas Eve. Even though you're surrounded by relatives and loves and laughter, squealing children and barking dogs, the sheer chaos of Christmastime, you'll imagine being there, inside Ruby's, and seeing them:

That one special someone who's missing.

We all have one. A parent or a friend. A sibling. A love from what feels like another lifetime. Someone who used to fill a chair at our holiday table.

Only, on Christmas, they're not so far away—that is, if you're at Ruby's Place.

If you're lucky enough to be at Ruby's on Christmas Eve, your memories will come to life.

It didn't begin to happen until after Ruby had passed. Once she'd gone, the place hobbled along for a while. Everyone had known for some time that it would close. But the closing hurt just the same. Death is always a shock, after all—you can't prepare for it. Nobody moved on. Not really. You never do completely move on from a love that digs down to the deepest spots of you.

Anyway, Ruby's reopened a handful of years ago. And now, *now*, in this resurrected Ruby's Place—Ruby's 2.0—one night of the year, on Christmas Eve, the memories are so real, they have skin. They sit right down beside you and order their own favorite drink.

It's the magic of Christmas, some say.

Even those who don't hold stock in such tales—those who roll their eyes and grumble, "Bunch of silly old ghost stories"—even they have to admit there's something about it. Some tingle at the back of the neck. Some whisper of déjà vu.

Even the naysayers come on Christmas Eve, hoping to bump headlong into a memory.

But, of course, Ruby's Place had a life before all this. A life that had played out during five different decades, when Ruby was behind the bar. Her regulars would have quickly told you that. Yes, the regulars. The ones who arrived like clockwork each night after work, the ones who came to tell her stories or to lean on her or trust her to remind them in the hardest of times that there was also something special, something that deserved candlelight, out there in the world. Something lovely that could still be had. Still other regulars came to celebrate. They came for birthdays or for retirements or for double-digit anniversaries.

Maybe, in the end, those stories that had played out under Ruby's careful watch never left. Maybe, somehow, they soaked into the bricks. Maybe *that's* the secret ingredient that powers the place. That gives it the air of enchantment.

This tale, the one that you are about to read, is one such story that played out while Ruby was still running her namesake supper club. A story about Ruby's best friend and favorite regular, Elizabeth. The woman the whole town said had the elegance of a movie star, with her polished ensembles and her perfect blond updo and the red nails that curled in such a feminine way around her champagne flutes.

The long-ago year in which this happened, Elizabeth was the age at which we all dismiss the possibility of a magical Christmas. "Pfff," Elizabeth would have said, tossing her hand dismissively at such an idea less than a month before this story's opening. "Christmas magic. Why, that kind of thing is for kids." She would have squinted to emphasize the crow's feet, to say, wordlessly, that there she was, fifty years old. It had been decades since she had made wishes for something extravagant or impossible to show up in a box under her tree on Christmas morning.

And yet, as our story is about to prove, it just happened to be the most unexpectedly special Christmas of Elizabeth's life…

1.

1978

Sullivan, Missouri. December. The month of velvet dresses and silk stockings. Of cashmere topcoats and beaded clutch handbags with gold clasps.

Mere weeks before Christmas, Rossi's was absolutely filled with women shoppers, each searching for a gift or something special to wear on a sparkling evening out. They needed to look impressive and polished at their husband's company party, or needed to knock the socks off an old beau who'd gotten in touch to say he was coming back through town, or needed something with flash for a New Year's Eve with a sweetheart.

And they needed Christmas Eve dresses, too. So many of them had to have something new for a Christmas Eve spent behind the neon sign at Ruby's Place supper club. Over the past twenty years, it had become the place to be on Christmas Eve—to see and be seen. To revel. To relish the closeness of a friend and exchange gifts. To indulge in a decadent sweet. To gather around the piano and sing. To fill the air of the evening with perfume-scented wishes. To dress up and dream of the year to come.

Elizabeth smiled at Millicent, a multiple-hat-wearer at Rossi's: salesgirl, head of the store models, buying consultant, etc., etc., pleased with her presentation of this year's holiday ensembles. At Rossi's, Sullivan's premiere luxury dress store, that was how a woman still shopped. She pointed to the dresses or the suits she favored, and then in a flurry of zippers and flapping price tags, Millicent collected the clothes, crisp with newness, hooked the bright silver hangers on a garment rack, and wheeled them toward the fitting room. The shopper was then escorted to one of the soft, plush armchairs, where Elizabeth served her both tea in a chintz cup and welcoming chit-chat until a parade of models emerged in the chosen outfits, turning and twirling and showing off the finer points of each—the leather lined pockets or the complementary fur muffs or the woolen coats that could be turned into a dress with the placement of a wide leather belt.

Yes, women came to Rossi's. They came from Sullivan, and they came from Cape Girardeau and Kansas City. They came from Arkansas, too. Oklahoma. Illinois. Some came with credit cards; those women couldn't help but buy the hat as well. Or the dyed-to-match pumps. Or the second blouse, because it was so hard to choose between the burgundy and the silver.

Others came with cash. Savings carefully sorted out in wrinkled white envelopes or leather bank books. Some tucked their folded bills inside their gloves or pinned them beneath brassiere straps for safekeeping. They came because Rossi's offered it, the fantasy, hanging in the front window. They came to be treated like someone who had never known what it was to have to wait to buy the dress, seventy-five cents under the mattress each week.

Those with the cash were Elizabeth's favorites. Inevitably, they would return home to find an additional item at the bottom of their bag, one that Elizabeth had slipped inside, no charge, when they weren't looking: the cut-steel shoe clips they'd admired and returned to the shelf, maybe, or the silk scarf with the peonies on it, the one they couldn't bring themselves to buy because scarves had to be woolen and thick and protect from the weather. A scarf had to be for protection, not for decoration.

Rossi's was an experience. The sort of which had been slowly disappearing. The ladies' magazines had long ago declared Rossi's ways passé. The finest stores from Fifth Avenue to Rodeo Drive had abandoned such practices. To Elizabeth, it was a sad loss. Life everywhere was becoming mostly self-serve. She declared it would never happen at Rossi's—and the women who flocked to her store proved there was joy, even still, in the old ways. A woman could get lost in it all, the feel of the store wrapping about her, the air as soft as angora. Golden as the oils in a perfume bottle.

Today, it was Betty Weber who was sipping cinnamon tea and trying to be convinced by Millicent's model.

"Pants," Betty murmured, flushing as she bit her

bottom lip.

"Roy will love it," Millicent insisted, winding her finger in a circle. The model sighed—she'd already nearly turned a hole in the floor—but nodded, and spun herself in a way that revealed the fullness of the pants. The fluid way they mimicked the motions of a full-length skirt. She put her hands in the pockets, shifting first to one side, then the other. Millicent was usually Elizabeth's best saleswoman. But she was struggling with this one.

"Roy will not love it," Betty assured her. She patted the curled ends of the hair she had long been dying blond as a way to conceal all the gray.

Elizabeth—the same Rossi who had owned and operated her namesake dress store for a decade—had to give her that. Roy, Betty's husband, was not going to love his wife in pants. *One of those*, she and her best friend Ruby had often said, with a roll of the eyes.

But Roy was also quite vain. Elizabeth uncrossed her arms and strode across the floor, her red pleated skirt fluttering above her black knee boots. She reached beneath the counter, tugging free a small gold box. One she'd picked up herself from the men's section of Graham's Department Store and set aside for this exact purpose. Elizabeth had seen this coming.

She strutted back across the floor, winking at Millicent before presenting Betty with the box. Her flourish was accentuated by the flap of the bat wing sleeve on her sweater.

"What's this?" Betty asked.

Elizabeth made a motion for her to open it.

"Silk," Betty cooed, touching the burgundy tie.

"And a pocket square? Nobody wears pocket squares."

"Roy does."

"He does," Betty agreed with a laugh.

"Roy will never miss a chance for the two of you to be the best dressed couple at Ruby's Place on Christmas Eve," Elizabeth said. "And you are going to be at Ruby's Place, aren't you?"

"As we have every year for more than twenty years," Betty agreed. "Roy insists on it."

Elizabeth fought a smile. The truth was, Roy had made a bet with his brother-in-law, Nick, that Ruby would never get her supper club open. And he had used his powers as city council member, head of the chamber of commerce, and leading citizen of Sullivan to lay every obstacle in her path.

He'd lost, despite his worst efforts—and had been paying for it ever since. On Christmas Eve. Dinner at Ruby's Place—on him. For all four of them: himself, Betty, Nick, and whatever plus-one the in-law wanted to bring along. A girlfriend, a casual date, a friend.

This holiday season would mark his twenty-third Christmas Eve dinner at Ruby's. Not that Elizabeth was counting. Not that she didn't revel in it every year, the sight of Roy having to eat yet another side dish of crow right alongside his prime rib and old fashioned.

"*You'll* love it," Elizabeth said, nudging Betty.

"Oh, now you've gone and done it," Betty grumbled, setting her tea aside and standing.

Her frown smoothed out as she said, "I'm going to take it."

"And stockings as well?" Elizabeth asked.

"And a pin to liven up my topcoat," Betty said, pointing.

Elizabeth carried the purchases to the counter, her boots clicking on the marble tile floor.

She tugged a sheet of tissue paper free from the thick stack behind the checkout counter. Her hands worked quickly as she tucked and folded it around Betty Weber's purchase—a suit of deep burgundy, satin pants and velvet jacket, with a white silk bow blouse. The snap and crinkle that accompanied her easy movements—she'd wrapped thousands of purchases since opening her store a decade ago—sounded to her like feet crunching in snow.

Elizabeth loved the snow.

Almost as much as she loved tissue paper at Christmas.

"I think this might be my favorite of all the Christmas Eve ensembles you've purchased," Elizabeth said with a smile.

"Well, I can't wait to see what you'll show up wearing," Betty said, pulling her billfold from her purse. "I don't know how you manage it, but you outdo us—and yourself—every single year." She sighed, picturing what this year would bring. "I love Christmas at Ruby's."

"Me, too," Elizabeth said, handing the purchases over.

"The music, the candlelight," Betty went on as the two women walked to the door. "The crystal chandelier. The—"

"Homemade marshmallows," Elizabeth added. "Those are my niece's favorite."

"Yes, those are wonderful, too. And your niece.

10

Angela. She's becoming such a lady."

"I can't wait to see you and Roy together this Christmas. I'm bringing my Kodak," Elizabeth said, the bell on the door jingling as she escorted Betty outside.

The cold air immediately poked through the tiny little holes between the stitches on her sweater.

She waved as Betty stepped into the stream of shoppers that filled the sidewalk, only to immediately disappear.

Night had fallen—it fell so early anymore. Dark before six. The streets overflowed, but not with hectic, harried faces annoyed with the burden of Christmas to-do lists. These weren't people just wanting to get home. These were people who relished the task. They shouted happy "Hello"s and "Merry Christmas"es. Shopping bags crackled. Bells rang. Carols competed with one another, bleeding through car windows or slipping out of store entrances. Car engines cried out their own melodic bass lines. Headlights washed the pavement in warm light. The air smelled of pine wafting from the tree lot on the corner.

Ah, December. The month of friendship and sugar cookies. So familiar and cozy, Elizabeth crossed her arms, shouldering the cold so she could enjoy the scene.

And then, unexpectedly, a face. Familiar, but also one that Elizabeth had not seen for forty years. A wrinkled face, now, surrounded by white hair. But those eyes. Violet. Elizabeth had only seen violet eyes once before.

Elizabeth held her gaze as the sounds grew distant and the shoppers flowed around both of them.

Just as Elizabeth composed herself enough to greet her, to tell her hello, the woman tucked her head down and was swallowed up by the night's foot traffic.

"Wait," Elizabeth called out.

She uncrossed her arms, the icy cold attacking her cheeks.

"Wait!" she tried again.

"Elizabeth!"

Her heart lurched. Had the woman called out to her? Did she recognize her? Remember her name after all this time? But when she turned, she realized it was Millicent, standing in Rossi's open doorway. Concern distorted her face.

Elizabeth glanced out at the crowd one last time. But the face—and the violet eyes—were gone.

She forced a smile, heading back inside.

"Everything okay?" Millicent asked. "You seem rattled."

"I thought I recognized someone."

"A client? A friend? That beau you insist you don't have?"

"No," Elizabeth said softly. She stood at the plate glass window, her eyes bouncing about the bustling street once more. "The woman who gave me the very best Christmas present."

"You mean, of your childhood?"

"Yes—no. Best present I've ever received."

"You're kidding," Millicent said. "What was her name?"

Elizabeth sucked in a breath and admitted, "I don't know."

2.

December, 1938

Elizabeth wasn't prepared for a knock at the door.

The back door, no less, which meant it was no doubt someone hungry and looking for help.

Elizabeth hugged herself, her fingers instantly reaching for the fraying tear in the right elbow of her threadbare cardigan sweater. Her heart knocked, too, every bit as insistently. At ten years old, she wasn't used to being at home all alone. She had only just gotten old enough to share housedresses with her mother, though the elastic waistband didn't touch Elizabeth's skin, and the garment hung on her instead like a shapeless feedsack.

Elizabeth jumped when the knock returned. What

was she supposed to do? At ten years old, she wasn't used to making decisions on her own, either.

She unhooked the metal latch on their wooden icebox, as though somehow, new items might have sprouted up inside the insulated metal walls. The iceman had delivered their block of ice not two hours ago—speared the shoebox-sized chunk with his metal tongs, hoisted it from the back of his motor truck, and shoved it into the top compartment of their box. He'd tipped his ancient tweed cap at her. "Ma'am," he'd said, with not a hint of sarcasm.

How wrong he was. *Ma'am, indeed.* Here Elizabeth was, wishing she could be wearing her more familiar play dress, the one her mother insisted she'd officially outgrown. Here she was, looking inside her nearly-empty icebox, hoping for a miracle, like some naïve child. But it looked the same as it had when the iceman had been there: whole milk filling only the bottom half of the glass bottle, three squares of leftover cornbread, and an apple.

Again, the knock. There was a pleading sound to it, somehow. It wrenched at Elizabeth's heart like it wasn't a knock at all, but the whimper of a stray dog.

Elizabeth's mother, Mary, never would have let anyone knock more than once. Never would have let someone linger there on the back step, the snow swirling, feet aching inside their cracked leather boots.

The knocks had come with increasing frequency over the past couple of years. Elizabeth's mother would swing their back door open, and there he'd be, some stranger, clutching his hat as he stood on their step, desperation in his eyes. They'd been the scruffiest of men—each one somehow dirtier and hungrier than the last, all of

14

them with black nails and beards like untrimmed weeds. Always, the current solitary man on the back stoop would nod once at Elizabeth's mother and call her "Ma'am," a title Mary had actually earned. Then the offer: "Chop some fireplace wood?" if he was younger and stronger. Or, "Sweep your front step?" if he was older and stooped over.

Elizabeth's mother would agree. Once he was done, she'd invite him in, take his hat and coat. She'd hang both in the mud room, right alongside their own things. As though the men's coats weren't covered in dirt and coal dust from the railroads and food and even a little mold at times. As though there was nothing grubby or ratty or wretched about them. She would sit them at the table and feed them as she fed Elizabeth's own father— turnips and roasted chicken and fried potatoes. A slice of her famous butterscotch pie.

Last fall, in the midst of raking leaves, Elizabeth and her father had found the carving. Her father had, anyway. Elizabeth had just been there to watch it. He'd quieted the metal scrape of his own rake out of nowhere, no longer impressed by the enormous pile that Elizabeth had succeeded in making. "Why'd you stop?" she'd asked, the air full of the smell of chimney smoke and decomposing sweet gum leaves. Her father had leaned the rake against the fence and reached his hand out to run his finger along the lines cut deeply into their white wooden gate: the outline of a cat, with long whiskers.

"Who did it?" Elizabeth had asked him.

"The men who come."

"Why?"

"It's their way of talking. A symbol. So the other

men from the trains know who lives here."

Elizabeth had raised her head, looking in the direction of the depot. Occasionally, she could see the puffs of smoke, feel the rhythm of the incoming locomotives.

She'd turned back to her father, squinting into the yellow autumn afternoon. "Who do they say lives here?"

Her father had chuckled at her, put his big meaty hand on the top of her head. "A kind-hearted woman," he'd told her. "That's your mother."

The knock, again, snatching her away from the memory and setting her back down in the lonely winter kitchen. Elizabeth's chin-length hair bounced against her jaw as she whipped her head around toward the back door. Could whoever that was out there see her through the window?

She checked the cupboard. One tin of King Solomon sardines, half a box of Sunshine crackers. The blue squat coffee can with the orange Maxwell House letters had a tablespoon left in it. Exactly one tablespoon. From the day the can was opened, each serving had been measured out with such precision, you'd have thought it was life-saving medicine. But that last perfect portion, that was being saved for Christmas morning.

Elizabeth turned toward the stove, which her father had purchased back when times had been better. The Crescent dual oven combination range with the white porcelain enamel finish. She'd been so afraid of having to strike a match to light the burner. And so proud, an hour ago, to have succeeded. She had envisioned her mother coming home, seeing the pot of beans bubbling. Taking her into her arms.

Of course she would. Her mother knew that there were no small accomplishments. She knew that when you were ten, all alone, in a housedress too big, with the dishes and the soap flakes and the ironing, given a page from a handwritten recipe book and told how to season the beans for supper, striking a match was as good as skydiving. Why, just yesterday, Elizabeth had still been young enough to be warned about getting too close to fire. That fear she'd been taught to carry was ingrained. And suddenly, today, Mary was giving her matches? Suddenly, if Elizabeth couldn't get the match struck, there'd be no dinner. Everything depended on that match.

Mary knew exactly how far she was asking Elizabeth to jump. And Elizabeth had done it. She'd landed safely on the other side. Or so she'd thought.

Now, though—the *knock*.

"There's no food," Elizabeth moaned. Only what they had for tonight. It had been six months since her father had lost his job as a conductor for the Missouri Pacific Railroad, and Elizabeth couldn't recall when the last time was she'd seen her mother's pie. Her father had been a day laborer for months, always working somewhere new. On good days. On the bad, he came home empty-handed. There'd been a lot of empties lately. Knowing how short they were on everything, Mary had walked three blocks that morning, without telling Elizabeth's father. Off to Edna Lightfoot's house to help with the extra laundry she took in.

Three measly blocks. Why couldn't her mother be here now?

Knock. Knock. Knock. Please, Mary. Answer the

door.

The round silhouette of a head could be seen through the thin white curtain covering the small window in the back door, the one outlined in little cherries. Elizabeth had embroidered the curtain herself. Her mother had warned her only perfect stitches would look right with that bright red thread. But Elizabeth had tightened her mouth, asked, "What makes you think they won't be perfect?" and had set about constructing tight, tiny little stitches, done with such painstaking attention that they appeared to have been made by a machine.

She thought about all this—the hours spent with the needle and thread, the heaviness of the iron as she'd made her hem, the *I'll show you* burn.

Now, here she was, a little girl wishing for her mother.

She couldn't open that door. She just couldn't. As soon as she did, whoever that desperate man was out there would be able to see the Crescent stove and the Perc-O-Toaster her father had purchased back when he was still a conductor. Those shiny appliances would make whoever that was outside think Elizabeth had something to share.

There was nothing, though. Not anymore. Her mother had scolded her two nights ago—her short temper so unlike Mary—for not wanting to eat her Brussels sprouts. "Now is not the time to be picky," she'd told Elizabeth. And Elizabeth had known: there was nothing else to replace them. It was eat what was on her plate or go hungry.

Elizabeth flinched. Another knock.

One week until Christmas.

A terrible time to be cold and alone.

A terrible time. The knock. Like a whimper.

It was torture.

And Elizabeth did it. She opened that door.

A woman stood on the back step. Elizabeth felt her head jutting back in surprise. They'd never had a woman before. Elizabeth supposed she looked to be about the same age as her mother, with a friendly smile and cheeks pinkened by the slap of wind. The knit hood that wrapped her head was stabbed with sticks and barbs, like she'd been spending time in the woods. Her wool coat had some tears in it.

"Please, Miss," she said, "is the lady of the house home?"

Elizabeth gulped as snowflakes swirled between the two of them. "No—just me."

"Ah."

Elizabeth hoped this would be enough to send the woman away. Who wanted to deal with a little girl? Most adults treated children with disdain. Like some sort of animals that needed to be trained and fenced.

And yet, the woman stayed. She stared into Elizabeth's eyes. They were violet eyes. Elizabeth didn't know such a thing existed.

"You wouldn't have a bowl of something hot to spare?" she asked.

"Of course," Elizabeth said, as she hoped her mother would have, opening the door wider.

The woman unwound her scarf. Elizabeth collected it and her coat and laid them both on top of their radiator, to dry them out.

It felt odd having a stranger in the house, even after all the men who had come. In truth, though, it wasn't the woman who felt strange, it was the decision. Elizabeth had never made a decision like this on her own, not in her entire life.

Elizabeth brought the woman a towel from the bathroom.

"These always stay warm, because we keep them in the cabinet next to the pipes," Elizabeth explained, wrapping the woman's frozen hands in it.

"Thank you," the woman said. Elizabeth thought she saw a tear in her eye. But she tried as hard as she could not to acknowledge it.

Elizabeth put her mother's apron on over her dress, and pulled out a square of cornbread from the icebox. She tugged the matchbox from the cupboard, too nervous about the woman's presence to be afraid to light this second burner. She placed the cornbread in a skillet with a pat of butter.

When the cornbread was warm, Elizabeth ladled out a bowl of navy beans and brought both to the table.

The woman slipped her hands from the towel. She gobbled the morsels in such a way that Elizabeth felt instantly warm in her heart for sharing it. She poured her the last of the family's milk. Hopefully, the milkman would show up too early tomorrow morning for her mother to know the bottle had ever been emptied. Her parents had made it a habit to drink water with dinner, anyway. As for the other missing servings, Elizabeth would tell her mother she had worked so hard, she'd had to go ahead and eat her supper before Mary could get home. She'd go to bed, letting her mother and father have the rest of the beans and the other two pieces of cornbread for themselves.

"Sit with me, won't you?" the woman asked.

Elizabeth dislodged herself from her place at the sink and dragged herself across the floor.

The woman was elegant, Elizabeth noted as she pulled a chair back from the table. Even ravenous, there was a kind of reserved way about her. She'd placed the bathroom towel in her lap, and she was using it as a napkin, dabbing the corners of her mouth.

"That was so good," the woman said, having swallowed the last bite. "And now, I must pay you."

"Pay me?" This astounded Elizabeth. Never, in all the times that her mother had been feeding the lost and the weary, had anyone ever offered to pay.

After all, if they had money for a meal, they would simply go to the city diner.

They pay in work, Elizabeth reminded herself. She tried to think of something the woman could do. Sweep the kitchen floor?

The woman reached into the folds of her garments. She wore multiple loose layers, surely in order to protect her from the outdoors. When she finally removed her hand, she was holding a ring.

Elizabeth got goosebumps when the woman passed it to her. The ring was heavy, made of a pale colored metal with a giant deep green stone in the center.

"This is platinum," the woman said, leaning over the table to point at the band. "These are white diamonds," she added, pointing at smaller stones circling the entire band. "And this," she said, pointing at the large center stone, "is a green diamond."

Elizabeth raised her eyes.

The woman smiled. "You know," she whispered, "that ring once belonged to royalty."

Elizabeth felt the bottom fall out of her stomach, the same way it did when she went down a hill too fast on her roller skates. "It's too much for just the food," Elizabeth said, pushing the ring toward her.

"No—not for the food. For your kindness. We reward the wrong things in this world—last names, tradition, external beauty. This Christmas, I want to reward something that's *truly* beautiful. Your kindness, in these times, so close to Christmas, when I needed it—that's beautiful."

The woman stood.

"Wait!" Elizabeth exclaimed, jumping to her feet as well. "Do you have anything else? How will you pay when you get hungry again?"

The woman only shook her head and reached for the door.

"Wait!" Elizabeth exclaimed again, and ran out of the kitchen. She raced straight for her parents' bedroom. She tugged the J&P Coats Hosiery box out from beneath their mattress, on her mother's side. And she pulled out her mother's money. One hundred dollars. All the money they had saved, in case of a bank failure.

"Here," Elizabeth said, racing back into the kitchen with her arm extended, holding the money toward the woman. "Take it."

"All of it?"

"Please. I have a house and blankets and soap

flakes. I don't think you have any of those things."

The woman's eyes sparkled. "No," she whispered. "No, I don't."

"Please," Elizabeth repeated with a nod.

The woman took the money. She counted it and returned sixty-five.

Elizabeth accepted.

"Merry Christmas," the woman said, through tears. "Merry Christmas—?"

"Elizabeth," she finished.

"Merry Christmas, Elizabeth."

Elizabeth snatched up the woman's gloves and head wrap from the radiator. "Merry Christmas."

The door opened. Wind swept the stranger back into the cold.

3.

$\mathcal{E}$*lizabeth* fidgeted as she heard her mother's footsteps coming through the front door.

"What is all this?" her mother called.

Cautiously, Elizabeth edged her way out of the kitchen. There her mother stood, in the center of the living room, all pink-cheeked and bright-eyed, tugging a snow-dusted scarf from her head.

"Doilies on the front hall table," her mother said. "The smell of furniture polish in the air." She was too happy, Elizabeth noted, to remember to remove her galoshes. As the snow on her toes melted, she began to drip all over their hand-hooked rug.

Smiling, her mother stretched her arms out at Elizabeth and hurried toward her. "My big girl," she cooed, pulling her into a hug.

Elizabeth's heart was heavy and cold.

"If I didn't know better," her mother said, "I would have thought you were trying to butter me up. But I know my girl. I know she's doing her best job for her mother."

She kissed Elizabeth's forehead. "How did dinner come together?" she asked. But at this point, she'd already let go of Elizabeth and was hurrying toward her bedroom. "Any trouble?"

Elizabeth tucked her hands behind her back and closed her eyes.

She waited. *Why was it taking so long?*

Finally—a yelp of shock. Or maybe disbelief.

The sound of her mother's feet returned—angry, this time.

"What is this?" Mary demanded.

Elizabeth opened her eyes to find her mother standing in the center of the living room, on the threadbare rug. The hanging pendant light—which was little more than a light bulb on a string—cast a garish light on her bewildered face.

In her hand, the cash box. Elizabeth had left it open on her parents' bed. The easiest way to break the news of what she'd done.

"There's money missing."

"Yes," Elizabeth told her. And swallowed. "But I have this." She reached into the pocket on her dress, removed the ring, and gave it to her mother.

As her mother frowned and squinted and held the ring increasingly closer to her nose, Elizabeth told her the story. Told it all in one breath, trembling, hoping.

When she was done, it seemed to her there had to be something she'd left out. After all, her mother was still angry. And it hadn't taken long to tell the story at all. It had seemed a bigger story in her head. Hadn't there been more to it when it was happening? Had she missed something?

"Just like you and all those men," Elizabeth tried to reason, clasping her hands in front of her chest.

"Nothing like those men," her mother scolded. "Nothing. I never gave them money."

"But she gave us that ring," Elizabeth pleaded. "It came from a palace!"

"Did she tell you that?"

"Well, no, but—" What was it the woman had actually said? Something about royalty? She couldn't quite remember now.

"Get your coat," her mother demanded.

"But dinner—"

"Leave it on the hot plate. It should be safe. Put a note for your father on the table. He'll have a hot meal. Girls who make poor decisions shouldn't get dinner on time. They shouldn't get to eat when it's still warm."

She handled Elizabeth roughly, taking her to the corner, where they caught a bus downtown.

The city was festooned with red ribbons and pine boughs. It was even worse, Elizabeth knew, that this had happened during the holidays. She didn't know what her parents had been saving that money for, not really. She had assumed it was rainy day money, but maybe not. Hadn't her mother been *tsk-tsk*ing with the neighbor about end of the year bills? Still more clothes that had to be purchased for their growing girl? Maybe it wasn't just-in-case. Maybe her mother had been counting on it. Maybe they needed that money.

But so had violet-eyes.

When the bus sighed to a stop on the square, Elizabeth's mother shot to her feet and raced down the aisle of the bus. Elizabeth had to scramble to catch up to her, which was maybe even worse than the rough way she had handled Elizabeth on the way out of the house.

Rosenbaum's Jewelry & Optician, the sign above a door announced. Mary threw the door open with such force that it had yet to fall shut when a straggling Elizabeth reached the threshold.

The entire front of the store was a display for their newest watches. And jewelry in glass cases. A couple huddled together over simple wedding bands. Another man leaned against a counter, needing his eyeglasses fixed.

"Help you, ma'am?" a man asked, smiling at Elizabeth's mother.

"Yes," Mary said, tugging her gloves free. "The family recently inherited this ring, and I was wondering what it might be worth."

"Looking to pawn, ma'am?"

"Or sell," Mary said. "You know how times are. If there's any value in it, perhaps it might help my family get through Christmas."

"Of course," the man said. "Do you mind if I take it into the back? Where I can get a better look?"

"Certainly," Mary said. "Take all the time you need."

As he walked away, Mary turned her disgusted, pursed lips down toward Elizabeth.

Had her mother changed her mind? Did she really think there might be value in the ring after all?

"You'll see," her mother said. "That ring is worthless. You might not believe me, but you'll have to believe him."

Elizabeth tugged her coat tighter. That look on her mother's face—so smug. Elizabeth had hurt her, giving away their money. And now, she was going to hurt her back.

It was how hurt worked. Tit for tat. Always.

Elizabeth kicked at the floor, but not enough to leave scuff marks on the pretty gray and white tile. She figured the hurt deserved to stop with her.

She sauntered up toward a woman in the optician section. She picked a pair of glasses up off the table in front of her. As soon as she touched them, she wished she hadn't. The little gold wire specs felt fragile. The earpieces flopped.

But the woman was watching her. Elizabeth had her attention. And if Elizabeth wasn't going to hurt anybody, she at least wanted someone to know how badly she felt about it all. She looped the glasses over her ears and blinked up at her.

The woman was old—the kind of old that meant she had time to spare. She wasn't in a hurry. There was no one waiting to be served a dinner. She chuckled at Elizabeth. "Are your eyes bad?" she asked. "Can't you see?"

"I can't see anything through your glasses," Elizabeth declared. "That's why I like them. I don't have to see what's coming."

"Oh, shoo, you," the woman said, taking her glasses back.

The door to the back of the store burst open.

The jeweler stepped through, with the ring in his

hands, his face ashen.

4.

"Where did you get this?" the jeweler asked.

"Where?" Elizabeth's mother repeated. She fidgeted with the top button on her coat. She glanced about the store, until she found Elizabeth, still standing near the woman in the optical section.

She shot her a look of disapproval and waved Elizabeth closer.

"I—" Elizabeth started as she stepped into place at her mother's side, but her mother stopped her, putting a hand on her shoulder. Her mother was in the midst of telling the jeweler a story. Or, more accurately, a lie.

"My aunt," Mary told him. "Inherited, like I said."

"Was your aunt wealthy?"

Mary shook her head.

"Have any ties to Hollywood, perhaps? A love affair with a crown prince?"

"Are you pulling my leg?" Mary asked.

"No—it's—it's marvelous." By now, the color

had returned to the jeweler's face. His cheeks were Saint-Nick-pink. "I've never seen anything like it. A deep green diamond. Five carats. A most unusual cut. Ma'am, gemstones with few or no inclusions are rare. Most jewelers will never have the opportunity to encounter a stone of that quality. And here I am, holding one such specimen. No inclusions! A rare gem indeed if ever there was one. In a platinum setting. I—I'm astounded."

Elizabeth could feel her mother's grip tightening on her shoulder.

"What's it worth?" Mary asked.

"Mrs. Rossi—you don't understand. I don't want you to sell me this ring."

"Why not?" Mary's face twisted. "We got it honestly."

"No—it's not that. I believe you. I do. But I can't pay you what it's truly worth."

Now it was Mary's turn to have the color drain from her face. "What *is* it worth?" she whispered.

The jeweler giggled. And then he shrugged. And giggled some more. "I don't know," he admitted. "Surely more than any person—or any business—in this town has on hand. More, perhaps, than you'd find in the vault in the Bank of Sullivan. Part of me thinks more than all the gold in Fort Knox."

"You can't be serious."

"I am." The jeweler glanced about the store, at the faces that were all now turned toward them. He cleared his throat and bellowed, "See here, Mrs. Rossi?"

He motioned for her to get closer. She and Elizabeth both took a step.

"See this mark?" He was speaking now in an over-ly loud, stiff voice. "That's why I can tell this is a fake. Nothing but costume jewelry. A nice bit of costume, per-haps, but—nothing but foil-backed rhinestones."

"But I thought you said—"

"That second look will get you every time," he an-nounced, putting the ring in her hand and leading her and Elizabeth toward the door. "Sorry I couldn't help you this holiday. But perhaps your aunt has other pieces."

The bell on the door jingled as the two women were ushered onto the sidewalk. The snow was falling harder now. When they stepped in it, it crunched. It sounded to Elizabeth like the crinkle of tissue paper wrapping a gift.

She loved the sound of tissue paper.

"Look, Mrs. Rossi," the jeweler said as the door fell shut. "That last bit was for the benefit of the ears in there. Hard times have hit Sullivan, and I didn't want any of them to get the big idea to rifle through your house when you weren't home."

"To rifle—"

"Mrs. Rossi, I meant what I said to begin with. I don't know where that aunt of yours got that ring, but it's special. I can't pay you what it's truly worth—can't even pay you half of what I think it's probably worth—and no one else nearby can, either. Not during these times. You need to put this someplace safe. Okay? Please. Sell it when people have enough money to give you what it's worth."

And with that, he grabbed the handle of the door and lunged back inside.

Elizabeth's mother swayed a bit on her feet. She

looked like the jeweler had struck her.

"Mom?" Elizabeth croaked.

Mary cleared her throat, clutched her coat about her neck, and took Elizabeth sternly by the shoulder. They marched to the bus stop. Mary's breath was raspy and quick; it rattled in her throat. She seemed madder than before, even.

"Where are we going?" Elizabeth asked.

"Home," her mother said sharply. "We need to get home before your father."

They rode back without speaking. Elizabeth couldn't understand any of it. Hadn't she done something good? If the jeweler didn't have enough money to pay her mother what it was worth, then she hadn't been foolish. She had given away their money, but gotten something far better in return. All they needed to do was figure out where they could trade the ring for the money it was worth. Why, the way the jeweler was talking, they might be able to buy a house and stop renting. They wouldn't need a cash jar on the fireplace mantel, that black piece of pottery with a lid, where her parents emptied out their pockets of any change, where they counted dimes and nickels until they could do something special, something even just for fun. See a movie, maybe. Buy some penny candy. Pick up a carnation for a button hole.

They wouldn't have to wait for anything. Not anymore.

Why was her mother so mad?

At their stop, her mother jumped to her feet and raced off the bus.

Elizabeth followed. "Mom!" she cried out. "Mom!"

But her mother only hurried on even faster. Kicking at the snow with each step. By now, it had to be more than three inches deep.

Inside, her mother removed her head scarf and called, "George? George?"

No answer.

"We beat him," she told Elizabeth with something that resembled relief. "Come on."

She raced to the fireplace, where she dropped to her knees.

"I'm sorry," Elizabeth managed.

"Sorry?" her mother repeated. "For what?"

"For you being so angry at me."

"Angry? I'm not angry."

"You seem like it."

"I'm trying to keep your secret, silly girl."

"My—secret?"

"Yes," she whispered. She began to paw at the bricks all around the edge of the fireplace, her fingers red from the cold.

One of the bricks clicked. Loose.

"There it is," her mother murmured, pulling it completely free.

She raced into her bedroom, returning a moment later with a little cloth satchel. The kind of thing that held dried flowers, that could be kept in a dresser drawer to keep the garments inside from smelling stale.

"See this?" her mother asked. She pulled the ring from her coat pocket. She dropped it into the satchel and put it in the fireplace, then replaced the brick.

"Get that coat off," she instructed. "Hurry. We

need to heat up the stove again. Get dinner warm. So your father won't think we were gone."

"But why?"

Mary grabbed Elizabeth's shoulders. "Listen to me. That ring is yours. Never tell your father it's there."

"But Daddy works so hard—"

"Yes, he does. He takes care of us. He's a good man. But he makes bad decisions with money. You hear me? Bad decisions. He bets on the black when the red wins. Every single time. If he knows it's here, he will pawn it for far less than it's worth. It will be someone else's good fortune. I can figure out a way to put the money from the hosiery box back. More laundry. Maybe piecework. And you can help. You can take care of the house while I work. Yes? But that ring, Elizabeth, that was something you did. That's your fortune, your smart move. It should be yours. It's your safety net. Okay? If anything ever happens to me, if I'm ever not around, that ring will take care of you."

5.

1978

"Did it? Elizabeth? *Elizabeth*," Millicent repeated.

"Did it what?" Elizabeth murmured, pulling herself away from the story.

"Save you. Or take care of you. The gift."

"I—" Elizabeth touched her forehead. "I'm not sure."

"You don't know?" Millicent said, frowning at her. "Did you ever learn anything about her, then? The woman? Did she come back? Once times were better? Don't tell me—she was some sort of queen, and she gave you a thank-you fee for holding on to that ring? Or you had some torrid love affair with her son, the prince?"

"No." Elizabeth offered a *get-real-we-both-live-in-the-same-world* chuckle.

"Do you still have the ring?" Millicent asked.

Elizabeth stared out her plate glass front window, toward the street outside.

"Must be a story there," Millicent observed.

"Yes, but I don't know what it is," Elizabeth said.

Millicent snorted a laugh of her own.

Usually, Millicent had a kind of sophisticated quality. But right then, Millicent was standing side-by-side with the face—still in Elizabeth's mind's eye—of the woman who had passed by. The shadowy woman, old as she was, still had an aristocratic air—just as the disheveled woman really had somehow seemed like royalty, there in the kitchen of her childhood. By comparison, Millicent now suddenly seemed like a paper doll. A flimsy replica of the real thing.

And that look on Millicent's face! Why, it was almost greedy. She'd gotten a little taste of something sweet, something unexpected, and now, she wanted more. Almost like a child. These details weren't enough to satisfy her.

Elizabeth felt her face growing hot. She wondered how she could have let loose with that story so casually. It wasn't as though she'd intended to keep it secret—Walter at the bank knew the story, as did her friend Ruby and a select few others. But the story was hers, every bit as much as the ring. The story itself was precious. And somehow, every time Elizabeth told it, she could feel a tiny little piece of it fracturing off, becoming a thing that now also belonged to someone else. It wasn't just hers anymore.

Oh, but this was all a bunch of silliness, brought about for no reason. No matter how familiar that woman had seemed, it couldn't have been *her*. Not the woman who had given her the ring.

Could it?

"Well, anyway, it's closing time," Millicent observed.

"You coming to Ruby's?" Elizabeth asked, turning the Closed sign.

"Of course. Everyone comes to Ruby's on Christmas Eve. But I was hoping to talk to you before I bought my own holiday outfit."

"No—I meant tonight," Elizabeth said.

Millicent blinked in surprise, abandoning for the moment her work of straightening the holding-for-pick-up rack behind the checkout counter. "You've never asked me to come out with you in the evening."

"I haven't?"

Millicent shook her head, slipping into her long khaki and blue plaid wool coat with the matching wide-brimmed hat. Her long mahogany hair curled perfectly along her shoulders.

"Well, it's high time," Elizabeth said. She slipped into her own topcoat—gray leather with a large fur collar. The smell of Cashmere Bouquet hit her nose as she drew the collar closer to her face. She had always worn Cashmere Bouquet. The scent was everywhere Elizabeth spent any time at all—her home, her store, even her car, the giant Lincoln her niece Angela called Oscar the Grouch because of its green color and the way the engine sounded like it was incessantly growling complaints.

Elizabeth locked the door of her shop, and the two women locked arms. They made their way down the sidewalk, toward the supper club that had long been owned by Elizabeth's best friend.

White lights had been draped atop window dressings. Lush red velvet ribbons adorned door fronts. Swollen gift bags took up most of the sidewalks; passersby turned sideways in order to give each other enough space to continue on their way. Elizabeth glanced up as Millicent waved to a shopper popping the trunk of her Plymouth, so full of packages one dropped to the ground as soon as the trunk lid swung open.

The Christmas Elizabeth had received the ring had not been a red and silver Christmas. It hadn't twinkled or arrived with a stack of wrapped boxes. It hadn't had a single red bow. It had been a brown Christmas, a dusty kind of Christmas, with a pine branch in a Ball jar of water on an old peach crate that her father had found discarded on the street corner and brought home. Her mother had covered the crate with the remnants of a white crocheted tablecloth and fashioned a few small newspaper chains to drape around it. Elizabeth had made ornaments cut from saved Christmas cards discovered deep in a drawer.

Her mother had found someone to restitch her father's work boots, the ones that had pulled apart at the seams, the soles falling off. She had wrapped the boots George had already owned for years in white tissue, securing the package with a snatch of red yarn. And when he'd shredded the paper to find them inside, it had been the delight of his life. Like seeing old friends. His eyes had brightened and he'd let out a moan of pure happiness.

Elizabeth had gotten a blouse, one her mother had lovingly stitched from the material of her own favorite skirt. It had been neither pretty nor stylish, but how Elizabeth had hugged her mother's neck when she'd seen it. They'd eaten potatoes and sausage for Christmas dinner. There had maybe been a piece or two of penny candy. A ribbon that melted on her tongue.

But the present that had meant the most to her was the secret. The one her mother had given to her, let her keep. The secret was even more valuable to her than the ring. Because it had been recognition that she had done something right. It had made her feel so grown-up. And it had been a special bond she and her mother had shared until her passing.

Snow started to swirl as Millicent tugged Elizabeth's arm. "We're here," she said, pointing at the bright green door and the Ruby's Place neon staining the night sky red.

Ruby's supper club was truly a club in name only, since the entire town was already a member the first time Ruby had ever flipped her Open sign. As the two women stepped inside, the crystal chandelier tossed sparkles across the room; linen tablecloths draped each table. Candlelight bathed the faces of diners. Evie, the official nightly chanteuse of Ruby's Place, tickled the ivories in her black sequin jacket. At the front of the room, Ruby mixed drinks.

"Hey, kid," Ruby called out to Elizabeth. Her nickname for her closest companion—a wink to the fact that Ruby was a good twenty years older, though the women both fiercely denied this fact in public.

"I'm due for a break," Ruby announced, motioning toward the backup bartender she'd hired to help her through the holiday season. "Meet me outside."

"Outside?" Millicent said, as Elizabeth ushered her back through the door and motioned for her to take a seat on the red wooden bench beside the Ruby's Place entrance.

"You can't be serious," Millicent said. Her mouth was still hanging open in disbelief when the door bounced open and Ruby emerged in a black wool coat and a red stocking cap, carrying three glasses and a bottle of champagne.

"'Bout time you brought Millicent by," Ruby said, offering her one of the three flutes she had pinched in one hand, moonlight glistening off the stems. "You've told me a thousand times that girl is worth her weight in gold."

Millicent's mouth wiggled as she tried not to show how much this pleased her. She worked hard at Rossi's. If Ruby knew that, it could only be because Elizabeth had bragged about her. She had, too—bragged that Millicent was possibly the best in the business at displaying new colors and latest styles in ways that made women's mouths water. Elizabeth had told Ruby all about the trip she and Millicent had taken to New York last spring for pre-season marketing shows. They'd split up, dividing their time between separate designers and distributors. *That* was how much Elizabeth trusted and relied on Millicent.

"Well, come on, Mills," Ruby encouraged, forcing Elizabeth to scoot down the bench enough to make room.

Once all three women were on the bench, Ruby popped the bottle and poured three glasses.

"Don't tell anybody I'm still on the clock," Ruby warned Millicent.

"Don't tell anybody she keeps a sloe gin fizz going under the bar," Elizabeth said.

"Snitch," Ruby grumbled. She leaned back against the bench, stretching her legs out in front of her.

Even past middle age, Ruby was lovely, her dancer's body still lithe and strong. Most said (only half in jest) that Ruby would celebrate her hundredth birthday working behind the bar. Just as some people could hold their liquor, not showing the effects of alcohol, Ruby could somehow hold her years, showing few effects of the hands of time. Her gray hair had been twisted into a bun on top of her head—the same knot she'd worn on the stage throughout her previous life as a ballerina.

Elizabeth marveled at the way Ruby could look graceful no matter what she did—even drink straight from the champagne bottle.

"What're we celebrating?" Millicent asked.

"Nothing in particular. It's Elizabeth's favorite drink," Ruby said.

"Don't lie to her," Elizabeth said, as a snowflake landed on the tip of her nose.

Leaning around Ruby, Elizabeth told Millicent, "This bench came from a pond over at old man Pendleton's place. Ruby here used to skate on it as a girl. Her aunt worked at the Pendleton estate, along with another woman. Ida. Ruby comes out here when missing Ida gets to be too much for her. Toasts her memory."

"Don't act like I'm long-suffering," Ruby scolded. "This is my first Christmas without her."

"The recipes here are all Ida's," Elizabeth told Millicent. "All the drinks. The hot cocoa. The homemade marshmallows. The—"

"All right, all right," Ruby groaned. "If Ida hadn't wandered by while I was in the midst of trying to renovate the joint, it would have been a much different story for me and this old club. She saved my hide. I was a retired ballerina who had no idea how little I really knew about a kitchen."

"To Ida," Millicent said, offering her flute in a toast.

"To Ida," Ruby echoed. "Saver of hides. Many of them."

"Many?" Elizabeth asked, once they'd all clinked their glasses.

"She saved my aunt's life once," Ruby said.

"Did she finally own up to that at the end?" Elizabeth asked. "Did you manage to wrench the story from her before she died?"

"Might've," Ruby said.

"You going to share it at any point?"

"Oh, when the time's right," Ruby said, and hummed a bit, liking the fact that she had a secret.

Elizabeth and Millicent shared a look that promised each other they'd do what they could to get that story out of her.

"Look at that," Elizabeth said, pointing at the red bird on a nearby sidewalk square. He hopped forward a few times and tilted his head, intrigued by the women instead of afraid of them. "Cardinals appear when angels are near."

The women stared at the bird, the taste of the champagne lingering on their tongues, a few faint memories lingering in their thoughts.

At least, until Ruby held her arms out in a *stop everything* fashion. "I'm really gonna do it up this year," she announced. "I just decided. In honor of Ida. A Christmas Eve like no other."

"Hard to imagine that it could be any better than it usually is," Millicent said, taking a sip of her champagne.

"That's the trick, though," Ruby announced, holding her finger up. "Everyone expects—what?"

"A Christmas Eve of splendor," Millicent said. "The piano music, the pine on the tables, the crystal chandeliers and the flickering table candles. The gifts and the closeness and—"

"This year, my friend, *this* year…" Ruby started.

"Pfff," Elizabeth said dismissively.

Ruby slumped into the bench. "What's gotten into you, kid?"

Elizabeth didn't answer. Just placed her hands in her lap and sulked.

Millicent wagged a thumb at her. "She's been like that since she saw that woman."

"What woman?" Ruby asked.

"A woman whose name she doesn't know, who gave her the best gift she ever received, which has a story behind it that she also doesn't know."

Ruby's eyes swelled and she turned utterly serious. "You saw her?"

"I'm not sure," Elizabeth admitted. "Maybe. I thought so."

"You already know about this?" Millicent asked.

"She used the gift as collateral," Ruby said quietly.

"For what?" Millicent asked.

"The shop," Elizabeth said. "And now, after ten years in business, there's no need for collateral. I've already paid back the loan Walter gave me at the bank."

"So—wait," Millicent said, putting the pieces together. "If Walter—Walter Drummond, VP of the Bank of Sullivan—allowed you to use it as collateral, then he had it appraised."

"Right," Ruby said.

"So—this thing is worth some significant money. Really worth money."

Elizabeth nodded.

"Wow," Millicent mumbled, and knocked back the rest of her glass. She held it out for Ruby to refill.

"Do you think she needs your help again?" Ruby wiggled her eyebrows.

"Not sure," Elizabeth admitted. "She'd be awfully old by now."

Ruby cocked her head. "You're serious."

"What—you don't think I could have really seen her? You think I'm hallucinating."

"Sometimes," Ruby said, "we bring things to the top so we can deal with them."

"What do I need to deal with?"

Ruby shrugged. "You tell me."

Elizabeth took a deep breath. "The woman who gave me that ring was desperate. She had nothing. And she still gave me that. When she didn't have to. I would have fed her for nothing. She knew that. She gave it to me for a reason. And Mom always thought that it'd save me, or bring something special to me."

"And it did," Ruby insisted.

"Did it? I mean, this should have been the greatest present of my life. Really changed something. But what happened, in reality? I borrowed against it for a little while. If that's all there is, it seems like a pretty weak ending to the story, doesn't it?"

"It sure does," Ruby agreed.

The women sat for a time in the cold, noses turning brighter red. Snow dusting their hats and coats.

"Then again," Ruby said, "it would make a *great* beginning."

6.

"A beginning," Elizabeth grumbled, heading down the sidewalk. She'd already said her goodnights to Millicent and Ruby, and now, all she could think about was that single word.

She threw her arms out suddenly, steadying herself as her boots slipped. The wind had blown the powdery snow off in places, exposing a thin coating of ice beneath. The champagnes she'd downed didn't help much, either.

The night was still, but her head was swarming. She couldn't shake the look of that woman's face. It consumed her. The starving woman who had come to her childhood door. The gift she had given her.

And the questions, sitting heavily inside of her: *I was given a glorious gift. What did I do with it? What can I still do with it?*

As she walked, she noticed that a few of the weatherproof ribbons dangling from parking meters now hung at crooked angles. The aluminum snowflakes the city of

Sullivan had been hanging on light poles for the last couple of decades were looking a bit tarnished and dingy.

She fished the keys to Oscar the Grouch from her purse. But she changed her mind and turned for her shop instead, unlocking the door.

It was dark inside. Shadows stretched from the racks all the way across the floor.

Her boots clicked as she made her way across the store. Had she thought this would soothe her somehow? Assure her that what she'd done had been admirable? It was a dress store. She was proud of it. But had it lived up to the gift she'd once been given?

She paused in front of her store's many ceiling-to-floor mirrors. She stared at herself, at her blond updo and her red nails, her smartly put-together outfit. What would that scared little girl in her mother's castoff housedress say if she could see her now?

Elizabeth pulled herself away from her reflection, slowly passing the headless mannequins she and Millicent had dressed earlier that day.

She paused at the large island in the center of the store, the giant square counter that held four different cash registers. Here, in the lead-up to Christmas, Elizabeth's seasonal employees spent all day punching in numbers—four lines of shoppers all at once, with barely a pause between each one.

She had barely entered the island when she stopped and gasped.

Because she saw it:

A man crouched low, trying to hide beneath one side of the counter. Above him, the cash register drawer had been jimmied. It was open, the lock clearly broken, the metal arms used to hold the bills down sticking up in the air. And none of the money she'd left was still inside.

He dropped some sort of metal tool, letting it clank against the ground. And he held up his hands, but not before he tossed a handful of cash at Elizabeth's boot.

***

Ten minutes later, a police cruiser pulled to the curb, its lights swirling.

The siren died, and an officer emerged, the street-lights bouncing off the metal badge on his hat.

He burst into the store, his weapon drawn.

"Oh, pffff," Elizabeth said, tossing her hand at him. "Totally unnecessary."

"I received a call for a robbery in progress," he told her, his gun still pointed, his knees bent slightly.

"You really look ridiculous," Elizabeth said.

"Was that a false call?"

"Oh, no, there was a robbery, all right. Or, really, the attempt." She wagged a thumb toward her cash registers.

The officer took a step.

Elizabeth raised her hand, asking him wordlessly to stop.

He did, reluctantly. His eyes darted about the shop, still trying to pinpoint the danger.

She motioned downward with her hand, asking him to *put that gun away.*

He shook his head no. But when Elizabeth stared

him down, he holstered it.

Elizabeth curled a finger.

He followed.

Together, they approached the square of checkout counters.

Rossi's attempted robber was quite young—still barely even any mustache to speak of. At least, nothing like the mustache the officer sported.

And he was tied up, a lady's lace-edged handkerchief stuffed in his mouth.

"Is that—pantyhose?" the officer asked, leaning forward for a better look at the fabric wound around his forearms.

The robber grimaced, struggling to find a more comfortable position. But it was hard, with his wrists bound together over his head and secured to a cash register drawer. Not the drawer he'd had a chance to break, of course. This drawer was still quite sturdy, refusing to let him go. His dirty sneakers squeaked on the floor as he squirmed, and the fringes of his blond hair were darkening with frustrated sweat.

The officer attempted to squelch a laugh.

"What?" Elizabeth asked.

"You tied him up with pantyhose!"

"It works. Obviously. Maybe I should sell you a gross or ten for your department."

The officer straightened, took off his hat. He was handsome, Elizabeth noticed despite herself. Kind of an old-school sort. Well-built. Tall. The kind of masculine guy that probably had a den in his home with lots of leather furniture.

"Sir," the officer said, addressing the man bound behind the counter, "I'd like to get to the bottom of this."

He reached down, untying the young man and helping him to his feet. After allowing him to spit out the handkerchief, the officer turned him around so that his back was to him. He clinked a pair of handcuffs on the would-be robber's wrists, and spun him back again when he was done. For some reason, it reminded Elizabeth of the way, just a few hours ago, Millicent had kept asking their store model to spin for Betty Weber. Back then, she'd been attempting to convince Betty Weber of the pantsuit. The officer narrowed his eyes, apparently attempting to convince the young man to confess.

"Nothing to say, there, son?" the officer asked. "I'm giving you a shot here to tell me if this was all a misunderstanding."

But it was Elizabeth who was in the talking mood: "I came in, and he was here."

"Just a few minutes ago?" the officer asked. "Kind of late. What brought you? Think you might have forgotten to set the alarm?"

"No, I—came to be in my shop."

He stared at her a moment, his face softening.

"That sounds stupid," she guessed.

"No, it—it's not." He cleared his throat. "So you own the store."

"I do."

He nodded. "My—uh—my daughter's gotten a few dresses here, maybe. I think? Do you sell to girls?"

"Rarely. Depends how old the girl, how tall. I do carry petite clothing. Sometimes it will fit young girls who have grown too tall for junior clothing."

"She's eight. Maybe that's a little young."

"A little. The last time I dressed a girl that young was back when I worked at Graham's Department Store."

"Where you got started, eh?"

Elizabeth shrugged with one shoulder. "Maybe she came with her mother, though?"

"Maybe. I don't keep track so much lately. About her mother, anyway. Since the divorce." He cleared his throat, as though all the uncomfortable feelings about his ex-wife had suddenly lodged themselves behind his tonsils. He coughed and tried a second time. "If she was here, she probably came with a book, my daughter."

This tickled something in the back of Elizabeth's mind. She did remember that, actually. A blond girl with glasses. A girl far more interested in her book than the dress her mother was purchasing. Most girls liked to daydream about a future shopping spree when they would be the one in the lush chairs, drinking fresh tea while dresses were brought out by Elizabeth's models. About makeup and handbags and the trappings of womanhood. Their first pair of silk stockings, perhaps. Elizabeth still remembered how it felt to toss her little white anklets aside and gently remove her own first pair of stockings from the hosiery box. How her heart had bounced around joyfully while she'd gathered the thin gauzy material down to the toe and smoothed it up to her thigh. How it had made her feel completely grown-up, right there, right in that moment.

"Geena," Elizabeth said.

"Yes! My goodness. Good memory."

"Pretty daughter."

This pleased him. He put a hand on the counter and leaned, almost like a man posing in a catalog.

Behind him, the perpetrator began to back up.

"You know," he said, "I've been meaning to come by. My wife and I split, like I said, and I would like to—"

"—get Geena something for Christmas?"

Elizabeth kept watch on the young man from the corner of her eye as he slipped through the door marked "Staff Only." That door led to an alley, she knew. But she didn't say anything. This was perhaps the best entertainment she'd had in ages.

"Yes!" the officer exclaimed. "I would like to get her something. Some doodad that would really knock her socks off. Even if she's not big enough for a dress, I could get her, say, a little purse, maybe, or a little pin or something. Do you have things like that? But it's just me now, you see," he went on, without giving Elizabeth a chance to answer, "with her mother off to marry someone else. And I don't know anything about those things. I think it could impress her, though, if I brought her something from here. I feel like, in her eyes, I might be in danger of officially being classified as an old fuddy-duddy. Maybe, if you have time, you might help?"

"I could help now."

"Really? But you're not even open."

"No—well, I'd be happy to help with that later, yes, but I could help you with this case here tonight."

"My—"

"Isn't that what you call them? Or is it an incident? What's the police code for a robbery in progress,

Officer—" She paused to look at the name tag on his uniform. "Barister."

He straightened up and glanced behind him. He held his hands out from his sides. "Where'd he go?"

"Out front," Elizabeth said, pointing.

Through the plate glass, the young man could be seen running down the street, his hands still cuffed behind his back. Elizabeth wondered how he could be so brazen. Why not keep running down the alley? Why run down the street in front of the store? The kid was clearly inexperienced with breaking and entering.

Officer Barister took off running, too.

"Excuse me," Elizabeth called, trying to get his attention.

But he wasn't listening. He was too busy running.

"If you'll wait a moment—"

But it was too late. Officer Barister had clearly decided to pursue this would-be perp. He sprinted through the store in kind of a flexed-chest run, knees pumping, nearly knocking down a rack of silk blouses in the process.

Elizabeth cleared her throat and shook her head as he burst onto the street.

The front of her store was nearly all window. And with the sidewalk empty and the streetlight shining bright, she could see the scene outside clearly. The two raced out of sight pretty quickly. Seconds later, Elizabeth put her hands on her cheeks and raised her eyebrows, shocked to find her robber racing back in front of her store again, this time in the opposite direction. And Officer Barister running by a few seconds later.

On the third attempt (running, yet again, in the original direction), the kid must have thought he'd lost the officer, because he stopped. Pitched forward a bit. If his hands were free he would have put them on his knees. He tried to catch his breath, his chest heaving.

Barister caught up. There was a scuffle. A strange one, in which the officer tried to subdue a would-be robber who had only his elbows to help fend him off.

Elizabeth sighed. She went into the back room to make tea. She hummed as the scuffle continued—as there were shouts and grunts. As a wrestling match took place under streetlights festooned with holiday decorations.

Finally, the entrance opened. Officer Barister burst in, breathless. Alone. The loser of the match, apparently. He slumped against the front counter, panting.

"I made you this, but you might need something more thirst-quenching," she admitted.

"Kid can run," the officer breathed.

"He *is* twenty years younger. Maybe twenty-five."

"You think I look that old, do you?" He frowned, straightened up. In a falsely lowered voice, he said, "Sorry I let him get away."

"Well, his license said he was eighteen."

"His—you have his license?"

"Of course. Why wouldn't I?" Elizabeth tossed the leather wallet on the counter.

"You stop the robbery, tie him up, get his ID, and still feel calm enough to make tea?"

Elizabeth shrugged.

"You want to work for the force?"

7.

Elizabeth walked with Officer Barister to his cruiser, parked beyond the entrance of her store.

"I'll visit the kid's home tomorrow," Barister promised. "Doubt he'll go straight home after that."

"Actually," Elizabeth said, "don't."

"Don't what—don't go see him?"

"I don't want to press charges. There couldn't be much in the way of charges anyway, could there? He didn't actually steal anything. The store is fine. Well, with the exception of a broken cash register drawer. He didn't even do any damage to my locks. You double-checked all the doors yourself."

Officer Barister seemed flabbergasted. "Still, though. Tomorrow morning, first thing. The parents should be home."

Elizabeth shook her head.

"But we don't know how he got in. If I go out there, it could deter him from trying it again, at the very least."

"You think he can't get enough of my pantyhose?"

Officer Barister eyed her, like he was trying to make heads or tails of her.

Elizabeth shivered as a few snowflakes drifted between the two of them.

"I'd like to drive you home," he said.

"I never accept rides from men who have yet to tell me their first name."

"It's Tom," he said, offering his hand.

"Elizabeth," she said, shaking it.

"Elizabeth Rossi." He smiled in a way that showed he enjoyed saying it—that it felt good to him, like the relief of strong hot coffee on a cold night.

And he still had her hand in his.

"Look there," Elizabeth said, as an excuse to slip her hand free. She pointed into the front passenger seat of the cruiser. "Louis L'Amour. Looks like the daughter got her love of reading from her father."

"I hope so," he admitted.

"A whole house of books," Elizabeth said.

"I'm building bookcases. Pine. The kind that can hold anything you put in them. The fattest, heaviest books. Geena's going to have a whole life of books. Her favorite store is The Page Turner. Across the street from that bar. Ruby's Place."

"Supper club," Elizabeth corrected. "It belongs to my best f—" Her voice trailed. Across the street, there she was again: a woman in a black cloak. That same-but-older face.

"Your what?" Tom asked.

But Elizabeth was edging ever closer to the street. Night and closed-tight shops and a new dusting of snow meant the entire square was dead now. Ruby's was even closed for the night. Not a single in-progress wrestling match was playing out beneath streetlights. Only a few snowflakes and ten feet of distance stood between Elizabeth and that woman. Surely she couldn't get away from her this time.

"Ma'am?" Elizabeth called out. "Ma'am?"

But just as Elizabeth stepped from the sidewalk, the black cloak was swallowed by the night. She was gone.

"You all right?" Tom asked.

"It was nothing. I thought I caught of glimpse of someone I haven't seen in some time. I have something that belongs to her. Maybe I shouldn't anymore."

"Now it sounds like you've done a bit of breaking and entering yourself."

"No," Elizabeth said. "Not anything of the kind. Merry Christmas, officer."

He reached for the door handle on his cruiser.

"I shouldn't," Elizabeth said. "I have Oscar—I mean, my own car. I should be going."

Officer Barister tipped his hat. "I hope we meet again," he said.

Elizabeth offered a nod, but she had no intention of ever seeing Tom Barister.

Christmas, though, had other plans.

8.

*I*n the first place, Christmas sent Elizabeth a crowd. The sort of crowd that pushed at the seams of her store, that sent Millicent nearly twirling the feet off every one of their models. Last-minute midday deliveries of tissue paper were required from the stationery shop on the square. "Nobody takes care of me like you do," Elizabeth told Denny, the shop owner who'd agreed to send someone her way that afternoon, knowing that flattery worked better than promises of paying a surcharge for a rushed order. She'd barely distributed the flats of tissue among her checkout girls when she realized she needed to place an order for extra shopping bags, branded "Rossi's" with a sprig of holly. The paper kind, with the twisted straw handles.

"Sure you can get those here in time, Roger?" Elizabeth asked, pressing her office phone still harder against one ear and sticking a finger in the other, attempting to block out the sounds of shoppers, even there in her office.

"It is a custom order."

"Of course, of course, for my best customer," the supplier had promised. "Just for you? I'll add in some extra garment boxes on the house."

Everyone was in the giving mood, it seemed.

After the flurry of a frantic day finally quieted down, Millicent and Elizabeth settled up the cash drawers together.

"Need anything else before I head out?" Millicent asked, picking up the zippered bank envelope. After the day they'd had, the envelope bulged, nearly pulling the teeth of the zipper apart.

Poor Millicent. She'd sweated most of her makeup off, and what had been a lovely Edwardian bun at the beginning of the day was now barely hanging on under the pins at the top of her head. Long spindly strands had escaped, trickling down the front of a blouse that also looked tortured—wrinkled and stained in spots from the greasy, mustard-loaded hamburger she'd dipped under the checkout counter to eat, a bite here and there, during the lunch rush.

"I'll get it," Elizabeth promised, sliding the envelope from her. "Go home. Make yourself some tea. Put on some Chopin. It'll relax you. Trust me."

Millicent had smiled, grateful. "Sure you don't need anything?" she asked again, though her eyes pleaded with Elizabeth to say she didn't.

"You take care of yourself," Elizabeth insisted, walking her to the door.

"You, too," Millicent said. "Maybe you should call that police officer to walk you to your car. He knows someone tried to rob you once. And here you are with that envelope of cash."

"I will," Elizabeth promised, even though she had no such intention. Elizabeth had given the pantyhose incident a lot of thought. An entire day's worth, in fact. She was absolutely not going to be held hostage in her own hometown. Especially not by some skinny boy in sneakers who could not yet grow a mustache.

She locked the door behind Millicent and set about shutting the store up for the night: turning off lights and double-checking the cash drawers for good measure.

And then—a knock.

Elizabeth jumped, her heart instantly banging about. Somehow, she knew that knock wasn't Millicent, come back to tell her one last thing before calling it a night. And she knew it wasn't a customer who had lost her billfold and needed to find out if it was inside Rossi's somewhere. It wasn't even the officer from the night before, stopping by to find out if she needed him to be her escort, as Millicent had herself suggested.

The knock wasn't even coming from the front of the store.

It was coming from the back.

Just like the knock from her childhood.

Elizabeth smoothed the front of her sharp black jumpsuit. It was one of her favorites; she'd had the waist tailored to her exact measurements. It fit her so perfectly that even when she hung it on the hanger at home, she could still somehow see herself inside of it. Its outline was a perfect match. It almost felt like staring at her reflection in her full-length mirror, but with her head and arms somehow made to be invisible.

Again, a knock. Louder. If a knock could ever sound annoyed, that one did.

Elizabeth wondered, as she had back in that kitchen of her childhood: *should I or shouldn't I?*

She didn't have to. It was officially after-hours. If someone needed her for an honest reason, they would have come to the front door. This was sneaky. It felt like they were hiding. Or about to pounce.

She gathered her purse, slinging it over her forearm.

Elizabeth had only just started for the front door— and Oscar the Grouch, parked right outside—when she heard it again:

The knock.

She stopped, standing marooned in the middle of her shop. The golden Christmas lights she'd anchored above her tallest racks twinkled, competing with the moonlight filtering in through the front window.

What if whoever that was out there was hungry? Or in need of her help?

"Oh, all right," she grumbled, tossing her purse on a checkout counter. She headed toward the back door, disabled the alarm, and put her hand on the latch.

She found herself wishing that this door could have a window in it, like the kitchen door of her youth.

But then again, Elizabeth reminded herself, *that kitchen door window didn't help you out much back then. The down-on-her-luck woman you found on the step completely surprised you.*

Elizabeth opened the door.

And there he stood, in the moonlight: the boy who had tried to rob her. His wrists still knotted together with a pair of pantyhose. When he saw her, he frowned.

"I thought you were different," he said. "They told me you were different."

When he lowered his hands, Elizabeth could see what had been drawn on his T-shirt:

The outline of a cat with long whiskers.

***

Elizabeth bolted from sleep, the blankets in a tangle around her legs.

She dressed in a pair of black slacks and a leather coat. She wished she had a pair of jeans. Or a decent pair of flat shoes. Maybe a pair of the tennis shoes Ruby favored. She wished she had something a little more youthful in her closet. Millicent had warned her a few years ago that clothes needed to be made for dancing—at least, where her younger customers were concerned. Fortunately, Elizabeth had listened in time for disco to explode. As for her own wardrobe, though…

Who was she fooling, anyway? She was never going to look like anything other than she was. A woman in her fifties—who was on her way—just before dawn—

—to the Willowing Acres subdivision. An older neighborhood, not exactly fancy, but homey. Quaint. Yards filled with large trees, well-trimmed shrubbery. Flower boxes under the windows.

The engine of her Lincoln growled complaints as she twisted and turned through the neighborhood, looking for the street listed on the driver's license in her hand. She steered clumsily, turning her head down every few seconds to squint yet again at the house number. Morning was encroaching. The streets looked gauzy and bluish-gray.

Elizabeth coasted to a curb, the heat from the vents blasting her as she stared up at a tiny little house. A kit house, maybe, intended to be reminiscent of an English cottage. Narrow pitched roof, rounded front door frame, stone steps. But it had been in disrepair for some time. It slouched, really, like a bored teenager. Shingles had blown off in spots, leaving bare patches. Paint was peeling, showing off all the different colors it had once been underneath.

The garage was a detached pre-fab structure off to the side, with windows cut across the single-car-width door.

Elizabeth cut the engine and walked up the gravel driveway. It was still dark enough that she could easily see the lights were on in the garage.

Elizabeth peeked inside. There he was—the same boy from the night before, seated at a work table. Michael A. Harris, or so that driver's license of his had proclaimed. Smoke rose from some sort of tool he was using, his lips moving as if he was giving himself instructions.

This time, Elizabeth was the one doing the knocking.

He jumped, turned. Frowned at her. Carefully went about placing whatever he was working on down on his table. It was an enormous table, one that filled nearly the entire garage.

She watched him slide from his stool and walk closer—what if he pushed past her and ran? Or called out to his parents, accused her of harassing him? Became violent?

He leaned down to grab a handle and raise the door. It sounded horrendous—all that squeaking and banging—and Elizabeth wondered how anyone on the street could sleep through it.

Once the door was up, there they were, nearly an inch apart.

"You got the cuffs off," Elizabeth said.

He shrugged.

"A regular Houdini."

"It wasn't that hard."

When she continued to stare in curiosity, he sighed, clasped his hands behind his back, and showed her how he'd squatted slightly, bringing his hands down behind his legs, then stepping backward over his wrists, so that his hands were now in front of him.

"I suppose locks are easier to pick once you can see what you're doing," Elizabeth said.

Michael crossed his arms over his chest. "What're you doing here? Show up to brag that you know who I am? Go on, you can send the cops out to arrest me anytime you want."

"I came to return this," Elizabeth said, handing him his wallet. "I told Officer Barister last night that I didn't want to press charges."

He eyed his own wallet suspiciously, there in her outstretched hand. As though he half-expected it to be some sort of booby trap.

"Why'd you keep it?" he asked. "Why wouldn't you give it to that cop?"

"Why'd you break in? Why me?"

He sighed, slipped the wallet from her hand and put it in his back pocket. All without checking to see if anything was missing.

He trusted her, Elizabeth noted. Or maybe was afraid to look.

He started back for the work table.

"What is all this?" Elizabeth asked, eyeing the wires and boxes and silver metal bowls that littered the table.

"It's going to be an amp," he said.

"An amp."

"Yeah. That you plug your instrument into. Or mic." He shrugged.

"Your parents gave up the garage to give you work space."

"Uh-huh." His response resonated with a *so what?* kind of tone. This annoyed her. He hadn't even thanked her for bringing his wallet.

Youth, she tried to remind herself.

"Why me?" she asked again as he plopped back onto his stool.

"I was out of cash. I was supposed to get paid last weekend, but I got fired instead."

"From where?"

"No—not where. From what. I was in a band."

"And they fired you. Why?"

"I'm really bad."

"You know you're bad, and you auditioned to be

in a band anyway?"

"Yeah."

"And they did hire you." This wasn't making sense to Elizabeth. At all.

"Yeah."

"I'm not a psychic, and I didn't go to dental school, Michael. I can't read minds, and I really dislike this teeth-pulling thing this conversation has going for it."

"Mike."

Elizabeth's silence indicated she was still waiting for her explanation.

"I make amps. I'm good at it. I think I could sell them. I have sold a few. Here and there. I thought—if I could get them onstage, get a regular gig with them, it'd help. And then, if I was in the band, I could talk to anybody in the crowd who might be interested in buying one themselves."

"So the band really just wanted your amps, not you."

"Right."

"Do they still have your amps?"

"Yep."

"So they stole from you first."

He shook his head at her like she really was clueless.

"Why didn't you file a report?"

"I gave them to the band. If they'd let me in."

"But you didn't specify you actually had to play any gigs when you made the deal."

"Lesson number one," he grumbled.

"Why don't you ask them to advertise the amps for you? Like you had planned?"

"Why would they do that? They'll sound better than other bands, which means they're the ones who'll get the local gigs. Why help their competition?"

He picked up a few wires, tossed them down next to his soldering iron. "If I had the parts enough to make one, things might be different. I've been out here the whole rest of the night, trying to make these odds and ends work. But I don't think I've got enough here."

"Why me?" Elizabeth asked yet again.

"You've got a lot of customers. And a crummy alarm."

"That's how you got in? You went around my alarm?"

"It was easier and quieter than throwing a rock through the front window."

Elizabeth offered a crooked smile. "Congratulations," she said.

"For what?"

"You just got another job."

He perked. "What?"

"A job. For me."

This deflated him a bit. "What do I know about a bunch of girly stuff?"

"No—you're going to fix my alarm. You do owe me." She pointed to his back pocket and the wallet she'd returned.

"I didn't break that alarm."

"But you said it was crummy," Elizabeth reminded him. "I want you to fix it so nobody can get in so easily.

And my door lock. And the cash register drawer you *did* break jimmying it open."

He slumped.

"I could knock on the front door, tell Mr. And Mrs. Harris how we met last night—"

"No, no, no," he said, holding up his hand.

"In the meantime—" Elizabeth dug into her purse and offered him a hundred dollar bill.

"What's this for?"

"It's an advance," she said. "And besides, it's all I leave in the register overnight, so we have something to make change with at the start of the day. It's all you would have been able to leave with last night."

Again, he stared like maybe it was a trick. Like if he tugged that money out of her hand, low and behold, he'd find one of those proverbial strings attached. Maybe even one that led to another set of handcuffs.

But the power of that hundred dollar bill was too great. He slipped it from her hand.

"Wonderful," Elizabeth said. "I have no intention of interrupting your studies, so we'll plan on Saturday morning, bright and early. I'll be at the shop by 7:30. Don't be late."

She clicked her way across the cement floor, toward the gravel driveway.

"Um, is that *this* Saturday?" Michael asked.

Elizabeth turned, shooting him a look of warning.

"Okay," he relented.

Before another idea had time to take root inside him, Elizabeth added, "Don't forget—I know where you live."

9.

"**You** have some sort of meeting today?" Millicent asked, tucking a sheet of tissue paper around a tailored tweed jacket. The jacket was being purchased by Alice Drake, who would soon place the package beneath the Drake family spruce, where it would remain until her daughter returned from college to unwrap it.

Elizabeth smiled at the loud crinkle. Oh, how she loved the sound of tissue paper at Christmas.

She was in love with everything, suddenly. With the way traffic lights were Christmas colored. With the seven-thousandth playing of "White Christmas" on the radio. She'd even laughed and shared well-wishes with a wrong number placed to the store phone.

Everything felt either right or repairable, thanks to her morning with Michael Harris. She had fixed that situation (a spruced-up alarm and repaired cash register drawer in exchange for a get-out-of-jail free card), and now, she was going to fix another.

"Meeting?" Elizabeth repeated.

"You seem in an awful hurry," Millicent observed.

"Just anxious to get going on a new project," Elizabeth told her, and began to hum a random holiday tune—a strange blending of "Jingle Bells" and "O Christmas Tree."

"Oh, yeah?" Millicent asked, her cheeks puffing out as she smiled at Elizabeth. "Got something to do with that unfinished story of yours?"

It did, actually. Elizabeth was going to put an ending on it. Tie it up with a nice neat bow. 'Twas the season, after all. Yes, she was going to figure out what she would do with that ring. Really do with it. Something substantial. Something meaningful.

Instead of answering, though, Elizabeth winked at Millicent and turned her attention elsewhere. "That's quite a jacket for your girl," she told Alice, smiling in approval.

"I hope she loves it. It looks so *collegiate*." Alice spoke that last word with awe. She'd never been, Elizabeth knew. College was a foreign land to Alice Drake; it glittered in her mind like the idea of Paris.

"She will. No doubt," Elizabeth said.

Being given a gift like that—a gift of value—was being told that the giver saw *you* as an item of value.

Elizabeth knew that firsthand.

"I'll be back next week," Alice announced. "I always come to Rossi's for my Christmas Eve dress." Then, leaning forward and cupping her mouth, she asked Millicent, "Has Mrs. Weber been in to buy her dress yet?"

Millicent caught Elizabeth's eye and nodded once.

She knew well the one rule Elizabeth had for her shop: *no gossip*. It floated throughout the entirety of Sullivan, but it would not cross the threshold of her store. To be sure, most of the time, gossip was told with a smirk and a giggle; it was good fun to be shared like a chocolate-covered sweet between the teller and her eager listeners. Occasionally, though, it could become something of a blood sport. And Elizabeth would not have it.

"I *heard* she's trying to get up the courage to buy her dress. That you've been keeping it on hold," Alice persisted. "Must really be something. Any chance I might get a peek?"

Alice's facts were smashed and mixed-up; Betty'd taken her pantsuit home the night she'd bought it. But neither Millicent nor Elizabeth thought Alice fully believed Betty's clothes were on the holds rack—more likely, Alice had mixed those facts up herself, hoping for the women at Rossi's to correct her, to dish on what Betty had purchased, so that she might have time to come up with a plan.

Clearly, Alice Drake wanted to outdo Mrs. Weber. Why, Betty's husband, Roy, had always been one of Sullivan's most prominent citizens. Owner of one of Sullivan's most successful businesses. Deacon of Sullivan's largest Christian Church. In charge of the charitable outreach for every group from the Fraternal Order of Antelopes to the Zoological Society of Southwest Missouri. He marched in parades. Attended ice cream socials. Still, after all these years, served as master of ceremonies for the annual Christmas tree lighting right there on the square. There had been talk of a run for office, something bigger than his city council seat.

And Betty? The women of Sullivan had admired her. Envied her. If not for who she was then at least for her status.

It would certainly be something—why, it'd be the joy of Alice Drake's current existence—if she could outshine Mrs. Weber. In front of her daughter, home from her very fancy, very glittery *university.*

Millicent and Elizabeth both knew that.

"On hold?" Millicent asked, cocking her head to the side and putting a finger to her chin, as though deep in thought. Not that she or Elizabeth faulted Alice for her attempt. But both women also knew that Betty deserved the chance to make her grand entrance.

Pants.

As Millicent feigned ignorance on the matter, the shop swelled with the orchestral holiday music that Elizabeth piped into her store all season long.

Alice began to fidget, feeling foolish, the awkwardness becoming painful. "Of course, I suppose I was—"

"Curious?" Millicent finished, attaching the bow to the top of her package. "Why wouldn't you be? Christmas Eve at Ruby's Place is quite the spectacle. I'm surprised the paper doesn't feature a best-dressed list."

Alice exhaled, accepted her package, and hurried away from the checkout counter.

"Merry Christmas, Alice," Elizabeth offered, reaching around her to grasp the handle on the store entrance. "I'll see you later about that dress. I'm getting a few things in on a late shipment I think you'll love. Perhaps your Rachel might stop by as well?"

"Yes!" Alice exclaimed, her cheeks flushing a deep pink. "We're so excited for Christmas Eve this year. What about you? Bringing a beau?"

Elizabeth felt her back stiffen, her lips tighten, her fingers try to fist. This, too, was a constant subject of gossip among the good people of Sullivan: Elizabeth's love life. Most were convinced she had one—a beau, that was—and was keeping him secret. Once, at the beauty parlor, her own hairdresser had declared (while Elizabeth was right there, sitting under the hooded dryer, no less), "Why, I heard that he's a movie star!"

"Oh, of all the ridiculous—where would I even meet—" Elizabeth had started, tossing back the hood and clutching the top of the smock fastened about her neck. She'd stopped, though, remembering the plumber who had recently come late at night, to repair her flooding bathroom. How amazed he'd been at her silk robe and the wine glasses on the table and the candles.

"Didn't mean to interrupt you, ma'am," he'd apologized, blushing like a schoolboy.

"You didn't interrupt a thing," Elizabeth had said, then realized: he'd thought she'd had a man over. She'd snorted a laugh despite her best efforts not to. "Those are my things," she'd said, pointing at the wine and the candles. And as for the silk robe, why, the best, most luxurious times involved dressing for herself.

He'd surely told his wife quite the tale when he'd returned home. Men in Sullivan often loved their gossip every bit as much as the women. More, sometimes.

"Bringing my niece," Elizabeth finally answered, sidestepping Alice's beau question.

"Ah, yes. Angela," Alice said. "Looking forward to it. She's becoming such a lady."

Elizabeth swung the door open. Winter air bled through her silk blouse.

As the door fell shut again, it returned, in her mind's eye: that green sparkling ring given as payment for her kindness. She hadn't seen it in ages. The last time had been when she'd used it as collateral. A decade ago. She itched to hold it in her hand. To see it with her own eyes.

She checked her watch again.

"Why don't you go ahead and go—wherever *it* is? The girls and I have everything covered here," Millicent told her.

Elizabeth offered her a proud smile. "I'm going to the bank," she announced. "If anyone needs me."

"Going to meet with Walter?" Millicent asked, pretending not to care if Elizabeth answered or not.

"Now, now, you know the rule about gossip," Elizabeth said. But she shared a knowing smile with Millicent as she cinched her coat about her waist, the chocolate brown frock with the feathered collar. In a nearby mirror, she adjusted her matching felt hat with the large brim.

Her heels aimed for the store entrance as she tugged on her leather gloves.

But she stopped, veering off to the side as a woman at a rack of skirts began to sway on her feet.

"Joan?" Elizabeth called out. She dropped her purse and raced to catch her before her knees buckled. In her arms, Joan felt small, and she gave in to Elizabeth's touch in such a quick way that it pinched Elizabeth's heart. Joan was such a tiny little creature needing protection.

"Sorry," Joan murmured, putting a hand to her gray forehead.

Elizabeth led the disoriented woman to one of her overstuffed chairs, sat her down, brought her tea and a few sugar cookies.

"Oh, the fuss," Joan grumbled, but she took a sip of the tea anyway.

"I'd ask how the radiation's going, but..." Elizabeth said.

Joan offered a weak smile. "I didn't think I'd still be this fatigued after treatment. I hate having to wait to see if it even did anything."

Elizabeth put a hand on the woman's arm, giving her a reassuring squeeze.

"I don't even know why I'm entertaining the idea of going to Ruby's this year."

"Yes, you do," Elizabeth told her. "Because you'd like to feel human and not like a Petri dish."

Joan barked a laugh. "It would be nice," she murmured.

"Two minutes," Elizabeth promised. She gathered some options and Millicent swept them up, whisked them off to the dressing room.

Models emerged, all of them twirling in the outfits Elizabeth had chosen. She'd purposefully selected luxurious fabrics that were also soft and comforting. Easy to wear. Complete with stylish but comfortable flats. Joan stared at the flats long enough that Elizabeth said, "Got it. Wait a sec," and raced to snatch up a pair of the tennis shoes that Ruby preferred, the same that Elizabeth often stocked for her friend. She gathered two strings of lace from the gift-wrapping station in the back, wove them through the eyelets, and hurried to present them to Joan with a grand gesture, bowing slightly at the waist.

Joan laughed when she saw them. "These just might help me get out on Christmas Eve."

"I'm counting on it," Elizabeth told her, squeezing her hand.

"You'll ring her up, won't you?" Elizabeth asked Millicent.

"Of course," Millicent promised.

As Elizabeth scurried off, Millicent shouted, "Tell Walter hello."

***

On the sidewalk, Elizabeth checked her watch yet again. She knew Walter's schedule as if it were her own: the timing of his mid-morning "daily constitutional" through the square, the hours he always blocked off for meetings, his lunch.

She would catch him in the bank now, before that walk of his, if she hurried.

She flipped through some of the ideas she'd had for the ring. She was after another loan, yes, but for something astounding this time. A second location that would showcase up-and-coming designers. Maybe even a fashion design school.

These ideas, she was aware, could very well require more than using the ring as collateral. They might require her to sell it. In a way, she thought, selling a piece of property you'd had for so long seemed so mundane, so less-than-magical. But she did indulge in a quick fantasy about an auction, one in which two attendees got in a rather heated bidding war, giving her a profit far larger than she ever would have asked for all on her own.

On the sidewalk outside The Page Turner, she paused, wishing she could see more than a holiday display through the bookstore's plate glass window.

And decided on a detour.

Silly woman, Elizabeth scolded herself. *Detours are famous for taking a person in the exact opposite direction of their destination.*

And yet, she went inside anyway, slowly strolling through the aisles.

Why would a police officer be shopping for books in the middle of the day?

Better yet: Why was she trying to run into one police officer in particular?

She turned, shaking her head, resuming her original trek. Inside the Bank of Sullivan, she removed her coat and hat, hung them on the hook inside the door.

She was about to head to the desk tucked to the left of the tellers, the one that held all the keys to the safe deposit boxes, when a man's voice called to her, "Looking smart, Lizzie."

The smile formed on Elizabeth's face even before she turned. She expected to see Walter, the only person she allowed to call her that. She could talk to him about her business ideas; he'd always been honest with her. And one of the first to champion women-owned businesses right there in Sullivan. "Walter," she started. "I—"

But when she finished that turn, she saw a police

officer. With a mustache. And a Louis L'Amour in his hand.

"What are you doing here?" she asked.

"Just came from the bookstore," he said, waving the paperback. "I saw you there."

"So?" It sounded far more flippant than she'd intended. She was only trying to sound as though she hadn't been looking for him.

Tom offered a smile. Saw through her response, it seemed.

Elizabeth caught herself smiling a bit, too, before she could stop herself.

"So, it seemed like you were looking for someone. Maybe me. Thought maybe you'd changed your mind about pressing charges," he said.

"Oh, no. No."

Tom nodded.

The conversation lagged—though they had barely said enough to each other for this to even be considered a conversation.

Elizabeth squinted at Tom. She couldn't help it. There was something about him. Sometimes, when you met a person, you could tell their strange, jagged edges would fit nicely against your own. She had not felt that in a long time.

"I came to see something," she admitted.

"I didn't know the bank had viewings," Tom teased.

"It's the only thing I have that's really worth stealing."

"Our Mr. Michael Harris certainly thought your

store was full of things worth stealing."

"Pennies compared to this thing."

Tom tilted his head, looking at her through the corner of his eye. "Now I'm intrigued. What is this thing, exactly?"

"Something of a mystery. Might I ask you to accompany me?" Even as she was forming the words, she couldn't quite believe it. Why was she asking him—a stranger? She might have told the story to a select few, but she had never shown that ring to anyone but Walter. Ruby hadn't even seen it.

"All right," Tom said, even though he was surely on the clock. Even though there had to be some issue pressing somewhere else.

"Lizzie!" Walter shouted, stepping from his office. "You coming to see me?" Walter Drummond, Vice President of the Bank of Sullivan, in his usual three-piece suit with the wide lapels, his large sideburns, and his outstretched hand. Walter was one of the few men Elizabeth had ever known to shake a woman's hand. Shake it like a man's, that was, like two equals doing business.

"How's that son of yours?" Elizabeth asked, just as she was always sure to ask. Behind Walter, on his desk, Elizabeth knew he had a brand-new picture of his son, Scott. He changed those frames out regularly—not only with updated school photos, but with pictures of the two of them fishing. Hiking. Camping at the Grand Canyon.

"Fantastic," Walter said, his eyes sparking. "Now you."

"Just signing in for the safe deposit. I'm authorizing Mr. Barister to come in with me."

"That's highly unusual," Walter said.

"But he's a police officer. It's a police matter," Elizabeth said. She leaned forward. "It has to do with official police business."

"Like a case?" Walter blanched. "Does this have something to do with that robbery of yours?"

Elizabeth raised an eyebrow.

Walter pushed aside the young woman at the front desk to retrieve the key. He took Elizabeth's. They walked past the vault, into the room of safe deposit boxes. Walter placed the two keys in Elizabeth's box, number 88, and pulled the box from the wall. He placed it on the table in the center of the room, and left, letting the door lock behind him.

"This place always feels so sterile to me," Tom said.

"Sterile? It's full of memories," Elizabeth said.

"No, it's not. It's full of documents, isn't it? It's a giant filing cabinet. Deeds and birth certificates and marriage licenses. Discharge papers. That sort of thing."

"It's grandparents' prized possessions. Their jewelry, their gold. All the things they worked their lives to acquire. It's the day your first baby was born. It's the house you bought for your family. Memories."

Elizabeth pulled out a velvet box and handed Tom the ring. "This was given to me by a stranger. A woman, who had lost everything during the Depression. I bought it from her, using my folks' hard-earned emergency mattress money. Thirty-five dollars. Even then, it was the tiniest fraction of what it was worth."

She watched Tom remove a pair of reading glasses from his shirt pocket and hold the ring up to his face.

"I suppose it's the robbery," she said, "but I can't stop thinking that I've had this ring for so long. Lately, it really hasn't been doing me any good. I should be doing something with it. I have some ideas...maybe I should back up a little."

Elizabeth launched into the story. The whole thing. Every detail that she'd shared with Millicent. "It's so strange," Elizabeth said. "I've shared this story with so few people in all these years. And now, you're the second person I've told it to in the last two days."

"You ever try to find her? The woman this belonged to?" Tom asked, turning the ring about and trying to get a better look inside the band.

"I thought I saw her. Last night," Elizabeth admitted.

"You're kidding."

She shook her head. "Isn't that foolish? It's been such an awfully long time. Surely she's not around anymore."

"You never know," Tom said. "Then again, maybe it's a family resemblance. Maybe you saw a daughter. A niece."

"I never thought of that." Elizabeth frowned. Could violet eyes be so easily passed down?

"What's the idea? Why come after this thing?"

"I'm not sure. Most of my life, it's just been sitting around, waiting for me to do something with it. My friend Ruby was the first person who suggested I open my own place. Told me to go talk to Walter. It wasn't until Walter mentioned collateral that the ring crossed my mind. All those years, all that time, I never thought about doing anything with it. Why?"

Tom turned the ring over in his hand. "Guess it's kind of like a stock you've owned a long time. It's hard to decide when it's right to sell. I've never had luck with that kind of thing. Bad timing. I'm the guy who sells off stock the day before it splits."

"I'd considered different ways of adding on to my shop, but now that I'm here, holding it, I wonder—is it narrow-minded to use it again on myself? My life is perfectly happy. Expansion doesn't necessarily mean more happiness. Could mean more headaches. Besides, even if I want to do some sort of showcase for local designers, I'd make money off it. It's not exactly selfless."

"You want to try to return it? Give it back to the rightful owner—even if, by now, the only people left are the family members of the rightful owner?"

"I'm not sure," Elizabeth mused. Who was the rightful owner? Elizabeth had paid for it. Even undervalue—wasn't that still fair and square? Then again, what if Mary had paid for something in those dark days—maybe shoes for Elizabeth or groceries for the week—with a family heirloom? Wouldn't Elizabeth want it back?

The ideas she'd had for the ring, the same that had energized her earlier that day, now felt like only the haziest of outlines. It was taking a little bit of the Christmas shine out of the air.

"I ask because it seems to be inscribed," Tom said. "Might have been an engagement ring or something. Are engagement rings ever green? What is this stone, anyway?"

"A green diamond."

"Ah. A rare gem," Tom said, looking right at her.

Elizabeth nodded.

"Sure is pretty," Tom said, handing it back to her. "It's hard to make that out, though, in the band. What do you think it says?"

They hovered together, their heads centimeters apart. Elizabeth wasn't looking at the letters, not anymore. She knew what it said. She closed her eyes and clung to it for a moment, the closeness of him. Let him sink in.

"Hey." He leaned in even closer to murmur, "You have to actually open your eyes to read it."

She cleared her throat. And she said what she had known about the lettering inside the band for the last ten years—the same thing Walter's appraiser had known.

"It's not an inscription," she said. "It's a maker's mark."

"*That* is, yeah," Tom agreed. "But this over here, this is an inscription."

"It is? What's it say?" Elizabeth asked.

"You've really never seen it?"

Elizabeth scrambled for her own reader's glasses. Tom glanced about, and picked up a magnifying lens left on a nearby viewing table.

"Here," he said, nudging her.

Elizabeth aimed the magnifier at the tiny cursive script.

"Can you read it?"

Elizabeth nodded, raising her eyes to hold Tom's gaze. "Take a chance."

10.

Michael was late for his first day of work. Which made Elizabeth furious.

So furious, in fact, she could hardly contain her anger. She hadn't pressed charges against the kid. She hadn't told his parents what had happened. She'd only asked that he be at her store bright and early on Saturday.

And here he was, standing her up.

Elizabeth wasn't really sure who she was mad at—Michael, or herself.

Michael Harris, she thought to herself. *Should have put him behind bars.*

She grabbed a fistful of Sale signs and headed out to the front of the store. She didn't know if she'd come outside because she wanted to take her anger out on the roll of tape that refused to pull free, or wanted to prime herself to tear into the kid the second he finally rounded the corner. Yes, even through her certainty that he was taking advantage of her, a sliver of her still hoped he'd show—it wasn't as though it was noon, she reasoned; in fact, her store hadn't officially opened yet. Still, bright and early, in her mind, meant before the shoppers showed up. He certainly could have assumed otherwise. Was he one of those kids who slept until the afternoon? She'd told him she'd be at the store at 7:30, but didn't specifically say that was the time she wanted him there. Had he misunderstood her? Why was she giving him excuses?

Why had she been such a fool? Why would any woman—much less a woman of her age and experience—decide to trust an eighteen-year-old kid who had already tried to rob her once?

She muttered to herself under her breath, hating herself for being such a pushover. To go to his house! Return his wallet!

She slammed one of her 25% Off signs onto the plate glass, and in a frenzy, began to smack some tape on the corners, not paying attention to whether or not the sign was even straight.

She was still in the midst of trying to rip off yet another piece of tape when she was tackled by someone on the sidewalk. At least, that was the way it felt. An out-of-control body ran headlong into her with such force, Elizabeth didn't think it was possible that any attempt had been made to slow down first. Did they mean to hit her? Were they not looking? This early on a Saturday morning, the sidewalks weren't exactly packed. It would take another hour or so for foot traffic to start to thicken. It wasn't like whoever it was didn't have the room to get out of the way.

"Hey," Elizabeth started, even as she was still

tumbling forward, struggling to catch herself before she whacked the pavement like a little girl, skinning the palms of her hands.

She righted herself, smoothed her pale blond hair into the chignon on the back of her head, and adjusted her plaid tweed ankle-length coat. Her fingers stung, already pink and aching against the cold; she should have worn her gloves. But gloves weren't exactly conducive to cutting off pieces of tape.

As she raised her head, she saw it yet again: the face from the past. Ancient now, the wrinkled face surrounded by a black wool cloak. Those violet eyes stared at Elizabeth—penetrating her very soul. Then they turned away.

"Wait," Elizabeth begged. She dropped her Sale signs and her roll of tape and started after her.

Each time she saw the woman, she got such a strange feeling. She was a child all over again, begging the world to slow down so she could catch up.

The woman glided with ease as she crossed the street. Elizabeth pumped her arms, breaking into a jog. How was it that she couldn't keep up with someone who was possibly as much as thirty years older?

The woman opened a store entrance, and slipped inside. Elizabeth's eyes darted to the electric sign over the door: "Weber Electronics."

"Great," Elizabeth grumbled. Roy Weber's store. *One of those*, as she and Ruby'd always said. If he saw her, he might very well chew her out for selling his wife pants.

Inside, Elizabeth searched the shoppers' faces. But violet-eyes wasn't there. Just Roy. And his brother-in-law,

Nick, surely come to help during the holiday rush. Roy always had his Open sign turned and his lights on before dawn the last few Saturdays before Christmas. A strategy few other shopkeepers felt resulted in any kind of benefit. *Who's out shopping before dawn?* And yet, they came for Roy. Elizabeth didn't know how he directed the crowd his way so early. And cagey Roy would never disclose any secrets.

Already, clumps of early-morning shoppers were checking out the latest televisions or stereos, both of which seemed to come in only the most enormous wooden consoles. A few were looking at displays of electronic games: something called Merlin seemed to be of particular interest.

"What's it for again?"

Elizabeth felt herself smiling. At least she wasn't the only one out of the loop on the latest gadgets. Merlin. Really.

"For guitars," came the reply. "You plug it in here, see—"

"Son, I can't see my customers having any need for something like that."

When Elizabeth followed the voices, she realized that original question, that *what's it for again* hadn't come from a shopper, but from Roy himself.

And the person answering is none other than Michael Harris, Elizabeth thought angrily. Heat cascaded from her flushed cheeks as she watched him twisting dials, showing off the finer points.

"Let me show you how it works," Michael offered, sliding a screwdriver out of his back pocket.

"No, son, it's not about craftsmanship. It's not about innovation or even whether I personally think it's a good idea. I can't sell it." Roy was looking tired lately, Elizabeth noted. His hair thinner, his stomach wider. Absentmindedly, he reached for the Pall Malls in his shirt pocket. "Why don't you try a music store?"

"I did, but nobody will—"

The staff door burst open; Roy's son emerged, waving to his dad, saying something about that delivery he'd been waiting on finally getting there.

"Then I don't know what to tell you," Roy said, racing off, leaving Nick in charge of the floor.

Michael sighed, looking utterly heartbroken. He hoisted his amp off the counter—it was a cube of no more than a foot in any direction, maybe even ten inches, but the way it dragged on Michael, it seemed to way roughly four hundred pounds. He limp-dragged-shuffled toward the door.

And stopped when he caught Elizabeth's eye.

"Think you were going to forget about our arrangement? Think I wouldn't notice?" she asked.

"What're you talking about?" he grumbled. He glanced about, at the shoppers who had turned wide-eyed stares toward the two of them. Embarrassed, he did his best to skitter out of Weber Electronics.

"Hey!" Elizabeth shouted, bursting through the door. Her voice traveled straight to Ruby's Place right across the street. Ruby was out, in her wide pants and tennis shoes, hanging a wreath on her bright green door. She stopped when she heard Elizabeth's voice.

"I've already been to your place," Michael said between grunts. He leaned even farther, taking lumbering steps.

"Stop. Please," Elizabeth said. "Put that thing down. It looks heavy."

Michael sighed, gingerly placing the amp on the sidewalk.

"I was at my store early this morning. Changing up the displays, hanging signs. All my girls were there. Why did no one see you, if you've been by?"

"Be*cause*," Michael said, "I worked on the alarm. Isn't that what you wanted? I was out back."

"You were—"

"I left a note on the inside of the back door."

"You guys need some help?" Ruby shouted. "I've got a dolly." Without waiting for an answer, Ruby dipped inside and came back out with a red two-wheeler. It rattled and clanged like it was trying to play its own joyful carol as Ruby raced it over to them. She took a step behind Michael, settling into a spot where he couldn't see her. *Is that him?* she mouthed in an over-exaggerated way. Because of course Elizabeth had told her best friend all about the young robber she'd found huddling beneath her cash register.

Elizabeth offered the slightest of nods.

Ruby smiled in that way that said she was trying not to laugh. She smacked the back of Michael's shoulder in a friendly way. "No rush bringing it back," she said, and started walking backward, toward her bar. She held a thumb and a pinky finger against her mouth and ear, asking that Elizabeth call her with this story later.

Again, Elizabeth offered the tiniest of nods.

To Michael, she said, "Well, come on. Let's take a look."

They were off again, Elizabeth and the young boy.

He dragged his amp toward the alley behind her store.

"That's not my alarm," Elizabeth said immediately.

"I know. It was a magnetic alarm," the boy said. "Those are easy. You can trick them into thinking they've never been opened. See, when the door opens, the magnetic bond is broken, and it triggers the alarm to go off. But yours I could open no problem, tricking it with a magnet from my fridge."

"So you bought me a new alarm, because you thought mine was no good."

"Sure." He shrugged.

"With what?"

"I was able to do a deal on some parts I needed for the new amp. I used the rest of the money you gave me on that." He nodded at the alarm.

"And you've already been out here this morning and installed it?"

"Yeah. That was the deal." He looked at her as though maybe she was already senile.

"I did leave you a note," he insisted. "It's right on the inside of this door. You'll see it when you go in."

"Okay," she said.

"Think your friend'll mind if I use her dolly to get my amp home? I've been lugging it around all morning. I was hoping I wouldn't have to take it back home, but… Weber—"

"That's fine," Elizabeth said.

"The instructions on how to use the new alarm are on my note," he said, pointing to the door.

"O—okay," Elizabeth said.

"Michael!" she called before he could get too far away.

He turned.

"Thank you."

The words pinched him. Elizabeth could tell. Because she shouldn't be thanking someone who had gotten around her other alarm. Because she shouldn't have to thank someone who was just living up to his end of the deal. Because he shouldn't have broken into Rossi's in the first place.

"And Michael!"

The dolly stopped clattering. He sighed, obviously annoyed. "Mike," he barked back.

"See you next Saturday."

"For what?"

"You've got a cash register to fix, remember."

"Yeah, yeah."

After Michael had rattled out of sight, Elizabeth went around to the front—both because she didn't want to trip the new alarm and because she needed to gather her signs from the sidewalk.

Elizabeth had finished taping up the last of her signs when a bus sighed to a stop at the corner.

"Elizabeth!" came a high-pitched shout.

And there she was—her niece. Angela. Hurrying down the shiny silver steps of the city bus. The Downtown Red line, or so it was called. Elizabeth had forgotten all about her coming that day. How could she have let all this silly business with Michael distract her? (Now that she knew Michael intended to fulfill his promises, the situation had somehow shrunk in her mind.)

Elizabeth laughed, opening her arms in time for Angela to throw herself into them. It had always been the way they'd greeted each other, all through Angela's childhood. These days, with Angela deep into junior high, Elizabeth made sure to savor the greeting. It would be gone before too much longer.

"You're going to help me come up with the very best Ruby's Place Christmas Eve outfit yet," Angela announced as she pulled herself away from the embrace.

"I like a woman who takes charge," Elizabeth told her, opening the entrance for her.

***

"Well, well, well. Is *that* what you're wearing to the Ruby's Place shebang? Listen to me, going on about dresses and doodads. But everywhere I go, everyone in town is talking non-stop about what they'll have on at Ruby's. It's an *obsession*."

When Elizabeth raised her head, there he was—Officer Barister, smiling at her as he leaned one elbow on the counter.

"That's *my* Christmas Eve outfit," Angela announced, puffing her chest out proudly.

"Is it now?" Tom asked. "Mind if I get a better look?"

Angela pursed her lips and squinted at him. "Maybe *you* can," she said, as though they were tight, two old friends, and not total strangers.

"This is my niece, Angela," Elizabeth told him.

"Tom Barister," he said, holding a hand out for Angela to shake.

Angela gave him that look all smart girls came by naturally—the one that asked, wordlessly, what his angle was. Tom fought a smile. He was already seeing it on his young Geena.

"Your mom around somewhere?"

"No. I came on the bus. I have my own account here."

"Independent woman," Tom commented with approval.

"I usually pick out everything. But Aunt Elizabeth always helps with Christmas. Because it's such a special occasion." Angela bent her arm at the elbow, letting her purse dangle from her forearm. She nodded once at Elizabeth, giving her permission to show Tom what she had chosen.

Such a show of wanting to be grown-up. Being so womanly. There she was, in her flared jeans and her platform shoes, long chestnut hair hanging in loose waves down her back. Could have stepped off the set of *Charlie's Angels.* But Tom figured she probably still had a collection of Skee-Ball tickets in that purse of hers. And he was right.

Elizabeth unfolded a winter white lace yoke blouse and a long olive green skirt. The skirt was tweed, not exactly a material for holiday nights—usually, women wanted velvet or charmeuse or satin to go to Ruby's—but it was the length that had caught Angela's eye. A skirt that went all the way down to her ankles was something special, especially for a girl who had spent most of her youth in short pleated skirts and knee socks.

"That's going to look beautiful on you," Tom said. "I look forward to when my own daughter's old enough to wear something that lovely."

"What for?"

"Because then I'll be able to shop for those things. I've never had someone to shop for before."

"Don't you have a wife?" she asked through a frown.

"Oh, I used to. But she didn't want me shopping for her. Think I might be any good?"

"Not as good as Aunt Elizabeth."

"So I hear." He leaned toward Angela. "I'm trying to convince her to let loose with some of her secrets."

"Good *luck*," Angela said, her eyes going wide in a way that said she'd tried herself, but had absolutely no success to speak of.

Tom raised his head to look Elizabeth's way. There was something in that look—admiration or interest. Elizabeth tried her best not to share a similar look his way in return.

Instead, she busied herself with placing Angela's "purchase" in a garment bag. Elizabeth had always told her she had a store account, like some of Elizabeth's best customers, but everything she'd ever picked out had been absolutely no charge to her parents. The bag Elizabeth chose was the sort that zipped, the kind she provided for the very best purchases, mostly formal wear. This time, she'd chosen it in order to protect Angela's new clothes from bus travel.

And still, Tom stared. Watching her every last little move.

Elizabeth grew increasingly uncomfortable with it. The last Christmas gift she would ever wish for was a man in her life. In her experience, men had been disappointments. Shiny packages that promised something grand and turned out to be a box of dirty socks.

"Dirty socks!" Ruby had screeched, nearly doubling over with laughter when Elizabeth had told her that, months ago, still dressed to the nines after a particularly disastrous date. (*Why*, Ruby had teased, eyeing Elizabeth's metallic long-sleeved dress when she'd first stepped inside the supper club, *you might even be dressed to the nine-point-fives*).

Elizabeth had frowned. "Can't you empathize with my pain? Here I am, having just had to ditch the most painful blind date of all time. I had to pay the coat check girl to pretend I had an emergency phone call."

A second round of snorting laughter had poured from Ruby. She'd put her hands on the edge of the bar to steady herself.

Elizabeth had glared before downing the rest of her drink.

"One of these days," Ruby had promised, wagging a finger. "One of these days, that won't be the case."

"Oh, men have been great friends to me, don't get me wrong," Elizabeth had said. "Walter at the bank has been your professional defender and mine. But romance I am officially moving into the column titled Things I Am Not Anxious to Repeat."

"Is that right," Ruby'd said, propping her elbow on the bar and her chin in her hand. Laughter continued to bubble inside of her, making her eyes water.

"Other things bring me far more joy," Elizabeth had insisted.

"Uh-huh." A giggle had escaped despite Ruby's efforts to keep it down.

"My store. My niece."

Ruby'd poured her more champagne.

"Your place on Christmas Eve," Elizabeth had gone on, raising her glass.

"One day, everything will be different," Ruby'd said.

Sure, Elizabeth had thought then, and she thought it again now, Ruby's words swarming through her head. *Different. How different can it ever be?*

"Can I count on you to tell me the truth?" Tom asked.

Elizabeth felt her stomach knot. But when she looked up, she realized he was still talking to Angela. He was asking *her* to tell him the truth.

Angela was leaning a little closer to him, her ear tilted toward him. She liked being depended on for information. At her age, adults never thought of her as someone who might know something they didn't.

Besides, it was always nice to get attention from a man as handsome as Tom. Had Elizabeth truly noticed how handsome the first night? Maybe a little. It seemed to her now there were celebrities not quite as good-looking as Officer Barister. How could she have missed that? *A robbery might do a good job of distracting a woman,* she reminded herself.

"Does your aunt have a beau?" Tom asked.

Elizabeth coughed, like something had gone down the wrong way.

Angela scrunched her face. "Like for her hair? A bow?"

Tom fought not to laugh—he'd had years of practice not laughing at his own daughter, Elizabeth supposed. It gave her a bit of a pang in her heart—most adults didn't ever censor their laughter around children. As though children didn't have the sense to know they were being laughed at. Even if they didn't know why, exactly, a child always knew when they were the brunt of a joke. And here Tom was, making sure to spare Angela's feelings.

Don't you dare go liking him, Elizabeth scolded herself.

"He means do I have a gentleman caller," Elizabeth said, zipping up Angela's garment bag. Pretending this line of questioning didn't bother her one bit.

"You're kidding." Angela made no attempt to censor her own laughter. "Aunt Elizabeth?"

"I'm not exactly covered in dust, Angela."

"I'd say not," Tom agreed. He nudged Angela. "I hear stories."

"Of course you do," Angela said. "This is Sullivan. Small town. You know. Gossip and all."

"But gossip is, occasionally, true," Tom said.

"That isn't. Not the rumor about her and the pilot. Or the one about the millionaire in Paris. Or the one about the movie star." Angela rolled her eyes.

"You don't think any of those men would take a

shine to your aunt?"

"It's not that at all—" Angela knew for a fact that Elizabeth was exactly the kind of woman who could draw men's attention. She'd seen it in restaurants and at red lights and on the sidewalk and inside Ruby's Place. She had always returned home to grab a pair of her mother's heels and practice her aunt's walk—that sashay that swung her hips about in a very Marilyn Monroe way. In front of the mirror, she'd toss her hand to the side with a "Pfff," like Elizabeth did when she'd heard something unbelievable.

But she also considered Elizabeth to be someone who belonged solely to her.

"Come on," Tom pressed. "Surely some of those stories are true. All those tales of male admirers."

"Maybe to begin with," Angela admitted. "A little. Then they get to be blown up." Now that she thought about it, Angela added, "She and her friend Ruby are both close-lipped about boys. Ruby had a love when she was young. But now she says he's in her supper club."

"No," Elizabeth corrected, "Ruby says the love of her life *is* the supper club."

Tom crinkled his face up, thinking. "That's not the way you heard it, though," he said to Angela. "Is it? You heard her love is *in* the supper club."

Angela shrugged. "I probably got it wrong."

Tom took a deep inhale. "Still. Lizzie here—"

Angela braced herself, waiting for Elizabeth to get after Tom for the nickname. Was utterly shocked when she didn't.

"No one," Angela said. Still waiting for Elizabeth

to jump in. But she didn't.

"Remarkable. A woman like that," Tom said, acting as though Elizabeth wasn't standing right there.

Angela bristled. "She doesn't need one."

"That's true," Tom agreed. "But then again, you don't literally *need* that blouse, do you? Still, it's nice to have it. You have something special in your life. And that's a nice feeling, isn't it?"

Angela glowered at him. She didn't like all this talking about her aunt. Especially when they were also talking about dressing up for Ruby's. She and Elizabeth had, for the past several years, gone to Ruby's Place on Christmas Eve. It was theirs. It belonged to the two of them. This man, this Tom person, who had started out being so nice to her, was now a threat.

Before Angela could figure out some sort of zinger that would send him packing for good, Tom turned to Elizabeth.

"I have something that would also make you feel nice," he told her.

"I don't think I like where this conversation is going," Elizabeth said. "Present company considering. Even *without* the present company, I'm not sure I like where this conversation is going."

"I have what you're looking for," Tom said.

"I've heard that *line* before," Elizabeth said, propping her hands on the counter.

Behind her, Millicent barked a high-pitched laugh.

But Tom was not one to be deterred. Or to even notice how outnumbered he was. "I have information on that name inside your—gift."

"You mean—the maker's mark? It's already been appraised."

"I think there's a tie closer to Sullivan than you're aware of," he told Elizabeth.

Tom grinned, proud of himself. "In fact, this information is so good, you're going to do anything to get it."

"Like what?"

"Oh, like have dinner with me."

"Is that right?"

"Yes." He reached for the garment bag.

"Hey!" Angela shouted. "That's mine." Quite the unsophisticated reply, but Tom's flirtations with her aunt had her feeling incredibly territorial and childish.

"I know," Tom said, draping the garment bag over one arm. "How about a personal escort home? No bus involved. We'll take my cruiser."

Elizabeth nodded, telling Angela it was okay.

"And you," he said, pointing at Elizabeth. "I'll pick you up at eight."

11.

Tom stood in the open doorway, stars behind his shoulder. In a blue suit the same shade as his eyes, no less. He was even wearing a tie.

Elizabeth took a small step backward—mostly out of surprise—and nearly tripped over the front hall umbrella stand. It clinked against the heel of her shoe and tipped, threatening to clatter against the floor.

Tom lunged, taking up Elizabeth's arm in one hand and the umbrella stand in the other.

"You all right?" he asked.

She blushed, which she hated. "Fine," she said, and her voice broke. Had Tom always been *this* handsome? She had asked herself the same question earlier, at her store, but...could someone actually get more attractive each time you crossed their path? At the rate this was going, the next time she saw him, she'd pass out. Like some silly old-time starstruck girl swooning over Rudolph Valentino.

She cleared her throat, chastising herself. It wasn't as though Sullivan had absolutely no men that could be classified as handsome. Why, even Walter Drummond at the bank still had that boyishness about him, right there, under the surface—that *why not?* kind of youthful dreamer's attitude that could make a woman lose herself imagining what possible adventures might be in store if she were to be by his side.

And still, as Elizabeth stared at Tom, her cheeks continued to grow hotter.

Tom cleared his throat, attempting to tuck his tie behind his jacket. His gesture brought Elizabeth's full attention to it. And now that she was staring, come to think of it, that tie *was* excessively wide, even for the standards of the day, and it was a kind of bilious yellow and green, with flecks of navy.

"My daughter picked it out," he admitted. "Last year's Father's Day gift. I couldn't say no."

"Is she home now?" Elizabeth asked.

"No—she came by for a while this afternoon, but left with her mother an hour ago."

"You could have changed the tie then," she said with a mischievous grin.

"No, I couldn't," Tom told her. "It wouldn't be right."

Elizabeth felt warmth spreading beneath her ribcage. He couldn't possibly be this nice, could he?

"Why on earth would someone leave you?" she blurted.

He smiled. "Greener pastures. Someone else with a bigger house. More interest in flying out to Cancun every holiday."

Boredom, Elizabeth thought. *Poison to even the loveliest relationships.*

"How is it that someone didn't snatch you up?" Tom asked.

She smiled back. "Too opinionated, too busy, too interested in things other than *him*, whoever *him* happens to be."

"So *he* says," Tom offered, still just standing there in her doorway. He almost looked like he was trying to decide something.

Elizabeth had wondered, as soon as she'd heard her bell ring, if she had overdressed in her black pencil skirt and her silver sweater with the cowl neck, the Eisenberg earrings and bracelet with the aurora borealis stones.

Now, eyeing Tom's suit, she worried that she was a bit *under*dressed.

"Here you go," he finally said, reaching into the pocket of his topcoat and handing Elizabeth a strip of paper.

"What's this?"

"The info I found on your ring's maker."

Disappointment sank in deep. "I thought— weren't we going to dinner?" She'd assumed he would give her the information after they'd gone out. Had he changed his mind about the dinner part? Why dress up? Had he gotten a better invitation from someone else?

"I didn't want to hold you hostage to it," Tom explained. "I'd like you to *want* to come to dinner." He pointed to the paper. "You can take that inside and shut the door in my face, if you'd prefer."

"I would—like to go to dinner," Elizabeth said.

"I almost think it didn't pain you to say that," Tom observed, a crooked smile on his face.

Elizabeth clicked open her purse and dropped the slip of paper into it, without bothering to unfold it.

"You don't even want to peek?"

"Priorities," she told him. She stepped onto her porch, shutting her door behind her.

Tom offered his arm and she took it as the two made their way to his car, still running there in her driveway.

And like that, they were off. Listening to Bing Crosby on the radio. "White Christmas" was suddenly new all over again.

"Where are we headed?" Elizabeth managed to ask.

"Place I always frequent at the end of my day."

"What's it called?"

"Cranston's."

Elizabeth felt herself tighten up inside. She'd never heard of it. She was going to wind up at some grungy bar. With a bunch of beat cops. *Cranston's.* What was that, the name of some former police officer who used his retirement to open a place where he could still meet up with the guys after work? They were going to all tell loud, embarrassing stories. They would pinch her rear and call her *sweetie.* Try to look down her cowl neck. She should have taken the slip of paper and sent Tom on his way. Only, that would be impolite.

You know that's not the only reason you couldn't send him on his way, Elizabeth scolded herself.

She was intrigued. Drawn. Though she didn't particularly want to be. Even when she had still been open to the idea of romance, she had never been the sort to fantasize about uniforms and alpha-males. Firefighter calendars, shirtless men on the covers of romance novels. It was all so unappealing. But there was something about Tom—the way he spoke about his daughter. The way he'd talked to Angela. Her niece had called Elizabeth earlier that afternoon to tell her Tom had walked her to the door, introduced himself to her parents. Made quite the impression.

Tom wasn't the stereotypical uniform sort. The kind who liked guns and his own authority. Instead, he was the sort to like books and people. So they couldn't be headed to some grungy old end-of-the-workday bar, could they? Especially if Tom was in a suit?

"We're here," Tom said, before Elizabeth had a chance to fully convince herself.

Elizabeth leaned forward to get a better look at what, exactly, that was in his headlights. A driveway? A house?

"Here where?" Elizabeth asked, confused. "This is a residential street."

"That it is. My house is right over there." He pointed to the cozy two-story next door, the one with the Christmas lights around the windows and in the trees.

"And your daughter isn't home?" Elizabeth asked.

"No, she's with her mother. Like I said. We have joint custody now."

Elizabeth hardened her face against him.

"Don't worry, Lizzie. That's not what this is about.

It's just that this is the best meal I could offer you."

He started up the drive of his neighbor's house, tugging Elizabeth away from the front walk. He pointed her through the gate to the backyard, then around to the back patio. The sliding glass door had been circled with a string of white lights—they were so similar to Tom's that Elizabeth wondered if he'd decorated this house, too.

Feminine cursive handwriting filled the sign taped to the door: *Cranston's.*

"My father used to frequent speakeasies," he said.

"Oh, really? That what this place is?"

"Well, it's a secret, anyway. Open to only the most select few. With a back entrance." He knocked twice on the door, paused, then knocked twice again.

A portion of a woman's face filled the crack in the patio curtain.

The curtain fell shut again just before the sliding glass *woosh*ed open.

"Helen Cranston," the woman introduced herself, holding out her hand. She was matronly, though Elizabeth was herself the age to hate such a description. She smiled warmly at Elizabeth, who immediately went about taking in every detail of this woman's appearance, as Elizabeth always did when she met someone new: her gray-streaked hair piled on top of her head, her round gold clip-on earrings, long-sleeved dress (belted), and her librarian shoes—the sort with low, block heels. Black. Recently polished. The belt was bothering her—Elizabeth could tell by the way she kept sliding a thumb behind it, as though hoping to stretch it out a bit.

"Elizabeth Rossi." Elizabeth performed a rather

pathetic, limp handshake. Had she been more in control of her thoughts at that moment, she probably would have been embarrassed by it. But all she could do, as she stepped inside, her shoes clicking on the olive green linoleum, was take in the aluminum-edged kitchen table decorated with candles and two place settings. The simple wallpaper littered with illustrations of fruit. The countertop cluttered with small appliances—coffee maker, toaster, blender.

Helen turned toward her stove. Elizabeth tugged Tom close. "What are we doing here?" she asked, ventriloquist style, shoving the words between her teeth without moving her lips.

"I told you," Tom muttered back. "Best dinner in town."

"How select is the few who have eaten here?"

"As of the end of this evening? Two. Two people will have eaten out at Cranston's."

He hung his coat on the rack by the back door, then took hers.

"Helen here took care of me and Geena. After my wife and I separated," Tom explained.

"Tom took care of *me* after my husband died," Helen said. "It was my pleasure to repay the debt."

"Kindness is never a debt, you know that," Tom told her as he pulled out a kitchen chair for Elizabeth.

"Oh!" Helen said. "I almost forgot. She slid something from the top of the fridge. Held it up to reveal it was a record. One of those compilations. *For Lovers Only*, the cursive letters on the cover proclaimed.

"Well, two lovers and one cook," she said. "I'm

going to go put this on. You two make yourselves comfortable. Feel free to pour the wine."

And then she was off.

Tom poured two glasses. He joined Elizabeth at the table.

"Ooops!" came a shout from the other room. "Never mind me! Just trying to get this old record player to cooperate!"

After a few more moments, when Helen still hadn't returned, Elizabeth said, "I don't suppose Helen is really having trouble with the turntable, is she?"

Tom smiled. "No, I don't think she is."

The two sat in somewhat awkward silence.

"Why are you so interested in helping me?" she finally asked. "It doesn't seem like you're only—"

"Flirting?"

Elizabeth shrugged.

"I'm not," Tom agreed. "I understand your feelings about the gift. The ring. How important it was—and is. How special it was for you to share it with me."

"You had a special gift?"

"Yeah," Tom said. "Not one I got, though."

"One you gave?"

"One I never got to give."

12.

December, 1946

Tom's dad Charlie was a cop.

This was a bottomless source of pride for Tom, who for years had worn his father's too-big hat during playtimes with the neighborhood boys. Who'd dressed like a cop for Halloween, without fail, each year. Who'd known, as soon as he understood what his father's job was, what he wanted to be when he was grown.

What the cold winds wanted everyone in Sullivan to know was that it was fully December. It whipped around corners and slapped faces. It tousled the snow that had begun to cover the streets as Tom walked down the sidewalk, toward Wolferman's Sporting Goods & Gun.

Inside, the store smelled like leather and wood

and men like Charlie. Tom felt a little small walking into a place like that all by himself. So many things on the shelves that he knew nothing about. Fishing reels and rifles.

"Hey, there, Tommy," Gramps Wolferman said when he caught the boy standing in the doorway, wearing one of his better pairs of dungarees. Not the ones he wore to play ball in over at the field behind the primary school.

Gramps Wolferman was not old at all—barely three years older than Charlie, in fact. But he had gone gray early; if high school yearbooks had been in color in his time, his senior photo would have stood out from the rest of the graduating class, looking instead like a misplaced faculty photo. And so it seemed he had been old for a long time. Since before he was twenty. The name, at first a tease, had hardened to concrete the day Tommy stood in Wolferman's. But really, didn't it sometimes seem as though half of Sullivan had a similar nickname? Anytime a child had a sentimental feeling for a man not in his own family, he attached some sort of over-the-hill title to him. It was a sign of affection. Or so Mr. Wolferman had decided.

Tom tugged at the front of his coat, wanting to smooth the hair he'd combed into place using pomade. But he fought the urge. Men didn't usually fidget with themselves so much. Grown-ups already knew that everything was in its place.

And Tom had come for a very grown-up purpose.

"I'm here for a gift for my dad," he said, his fingers worrying the coins in his pocket. The allowance money he'd been saving. It was the first time he'd gone shopping for his dad on his own.

This particular Christmas, Tom was eleven years old. Which meant he considered himself to be older than he was, and Gramps Wolferman considered him to be much younger—and less capable—than he was.

"What're you after, son?" Wolferman asked. "Maybe a lure?" He tried to steer the boy toward the fishing section. They had some beauties; young Tom gave Wolferman that. The sort with glass eyes. Just the kind of thing that Charlie would like. And well within Tom's price range.

It figured that Wolferman would come up with something like that. But then, the entirety of Sullivan was always trying to please Charlie, impress him. Charlie had been a beat cop going all the way back to the time of Prohibition and speakeasies. The people of Sullivan knew, from those days, that Charlie was not a brutal authority figure, a nightstick, a threat. Not the kind to run from, to fear.

Charlie was the kind of person who sought to make the world a fair place.

When he was with his father, Tom had often seen men tip their hats and women smile. Occasionally, Charlie was pulled to the side and spoken to in a hushed tone.

It was a special thing to walk the streets of Sullivan as Charlie Barister's son. Tom was beginning to understand that with greater clarity now, here at this strange seesaw of an age, one that constantly teetered between boyhood and the next phase, the one that angled now ever-so-slightly toward adulthood.

Tom watched Gramps Wolferman doing the math

in his mind. Rubbing his chin, he pointed his eyes toward the ceiling and wiggled his lips as he tried to figure out the right discount. For Tom only—the Barister discount. Might even throw in some line along with it.

But Tom was eleven. And he hoped, in his dungarees, he looked like someone fully capable of choosing his own gift.

Tom cleared his throat. Shoved his chest out.

Gramps Wolferman stopped his mental mathematics. "What is it, son?"

Tom pointed.

Wolferman looked in the direction, then smiled upon Tom. "Of course," he said. "I should have known."

The two walked to the baseball gloves. Always the salesman, Wolferman pulled two from the shelf, but Tom wouldn't have it. The money in his pocket wasn't nearly enough, and besides, this was supposed to be a gift for his father.

There were still many months of catch left. Not years, not anymore—Tom was eleven, after all. He was a seesaw angled toward a life of girls and high school and cars. He knew that. But he wasn't in the same kind of hurry as the other boys; he still wanted a game of catch. Out in the front yard, in the shifting, rippling shade of the pin oaks, surrounded by the barking dogs and the kids laughing and the metallic whisk and thunk of nearby roller skates. Car horns and shouts and waving neighbors.

There was still time. Not a lot, maybe, but enough to enjoy. Tom and his dad. Charlie's glove was looking ratty, Tom had noticed lately. Only made sense. It was a lot older than Tom's.

Wolferman rang Tom up, the bell on his cash register sounding like an impromptu Christmas carol of its own, and he made sure the glove was gift wrapped before he slid it into a shopping bag. "You tell your mother hello for me, too," Wolferman said.

Tom felt slightly taller walking out into the late afternoon. The snow had slacked off, the last few flakes twirling like ballet dancers. He smiled as he walked. He had something special, something for his father. Charlie Barister.

And it was almost Christmas.

He turned toward his neighborhood. He lived in a slightly older section of town, marked with two four-foot tall concrete pillars on each side of his street.

It had always been a comforting thing, turning past those pillars to see his house. Today, though, neighbors shoveling snow or cleaning off windshields stopped when they saw him. Then turned their backs as if afraid to speak to him.

He dragged his feet along, glancing first at one side of the street and then the other. They were all turning, showing him the backs of their heads, their shoulders. A couple of boys took steps backward. Mrs. Hannover wiped at the corner of her eye, her lip quivering. What had happened? What was he about to walk into? He got the urge to drop his package and run away. But where? From his own street?

Outside his house, he saw the large rounded curves and bumpers of a police car. His father was home. Charlie. *That'll make everyone stop whatever this is they have going on. That'll make them quit staring in that way.* Charlie

Barister always changed everything. Just by being around.

Tom was glad Gramps Wolferman had wrapped his present. It meant his dad wouldn't be able to see it. Not even when he tackled him in the front yard like he always did, grabbing him up and tossing him over his shoulder. Even if it fell out of the bag or Charlie snatched it up before Tom could stop him, eager to see what Tom had gotten all gussied up to buy. Even then, he wouldn't be able to tell what it was. Not all wrapped up in a box.

As Tom got closer to his house, though, two more police cars pulled up.

He hurried forward.

His mother was on the step. In her housedress and an apron, even though it was too cold for shirtsleeves. And even though she always took the time to untie her soiled aprons before opening the door.

Two officers were already talking to her, and still more officers got out of the just-arrived cruisers. The looks on their faces—the same as his mother's—and the neighbors'.

Tom clutched his package—the glove. The games of catch.

Time wasn't merely short anymore.

Time, Tom knew, had run out.

13.

1978

"Tom's dad was a hero," Helen chimed in, her voice echoing through the back of her kitchen, near the stove. Her carving knife clanked as she plated two suppers.

"Died in the line of duty," Elizabeth said, staring at Tom.

He nodded, the candlelight flickering over his face.

"He saved someone," Elizabeth guessed.

"It was an armed robbery. He saved the robber," Tom said.

"Wait," Elizabeth said. "You mean he saved someone during the course of an attempted robbery. Someone who was being robbed."

"No, he saved the robber," Helen chimed in. "Maxwell Ross. Been up to no good in Sullivan for ages."

"He was shot *by* the robber?" Elizabeth pressed.

"No, he took Maxwell's bullet. The one meant for him," Tom said, picking up his wineglass and taking a long, even sip.

"Charlie had his own ideas of good and bad," Helen told her. "Maxwell had already gone to jail once. And some of that was Charlie's doing. Poor Charlie didn't ever feel like he'd quite handled that whole situation right. Carried guilt about it. And when the time came to do right by Maxwell—even if he *was* in the midst of robbing someone—he did it. He took his bullet. So he could have another chance."

"Did he change?" Elizabeth asked. "Maxwell?"

Tom inhaled and shook his head.

"Such a sad story," Helen mumbled. "I hope it doesn't leave a sour taste on your tongue."

She carried two plates to the table.

"Is that Beef Wellington?" Elizabeth asked.

"It is at that," Helen said proudly.

Elizabeth took a first bite and shot a wide-eyed look at Tom.

"What is it?" he asked.

She swallowed, sighed. "It is by far the best meal served in all of Sullivan," she said.

"Helen, please," Elizabeth said, pointing at another chair at the table. "Join us."

"Oh, no. I didn't want to intrude. This is for you two—"

"This is too good for the cook not to enjoy. Please," Elizabeth said, pointing again at the chair.

"I'd like you to, too, Helen," Tom said. "You've outdone yourself."

Beaming, Helen skittered off to the stove, made a plate for herself, and joined the two at her kitchen table.

Tom poured her a glass, and Helen raised it as though to propose a toast. "To first dates!" she declared.

Tom and Elizabeth laughed, picking up their glasses and clinking them against Helen's.

It was, Elizabeth thought, as their laughter added a harmony to the instrumental record that played on in the other room, the strangest first date she'd ever been on.

If that's what it even was—a date.

She found herself wanting it to be one.

Mostly, she wanted it to be one because it would mean something. It would be special. It *should* be special. Shouldn't it? She loved everything about this evening. She loved where they were. She loved how good the meal tasted. She loved that Tom had dressed for her, all so the two of them could sit in his neighbor's kitchen. She loved that she had some sort of secret tucked away in her pocketbook, something about her ring, written in Tom's handwriting. She loved how comfortable she was and how sweet it was and—

"Well," Tom said, interrupting her thoughts, "there's more to my story. Which is really the reason why I understand about your ring. And it's not as sad as the first part."

14.

December, 1946

That Christmas Eve was far from magical for the young boy who had suddenly lost his father.

The star on top of the tree didn't sparkle. The displays in the front windows of stores didn't shine. And the cards on the mantle seemed flat and fake.

That last one—his sudden distaste for Christmas cards—showed how heartbroken Tom was. He loved Christmas cards. Usually. Loved sitting at the coffee table and addressing them with his mother while listening to their favorite radio programs. Now, he wanted nothing to do with the cards. With well-wishes. With Christmas.

Tom didn't want anything. The idea of having to open presents the next morning gave him a stomachache.

He knew that more than half of the presents waiting for him under the tree had been purchased by Charlie. He couldn't stand the thought of ripping the paper off—paper Charlie had folded and taped himself. And he couldn't stand the thought of looking inside, seeing what Charlie had bought him. Because he would see him, in his mind's eye, walking the aisles, whistling carols. And he would look at Charlie's living room chair, and it would be empty, and the worn-flat dents from his back and his arms would still be there. Tom had a pretty good idea what was in most of the boxes. Books and models. New tracks for his train set. How was Tom supposed to enjoy any of it when he had dents in his heart—the same shape and size as the worn-flat spots in Charlie's old chair? And no Charlie?

Was he supposed to go on, enjoy those gifts, pretend like everything could go on like usual? The world was stained a different color. There was no filling any gaping hole—even the attempt, Tom thought, would hurt.

He tugged his chenille blanket up, high enough to cover his ear. He hoped it would block any sounds of joy—carolers or horns honking, laughter on the street.

"I hate Christmas," Tom murmured.

"You don't mean that," a familiar voice said, tugging the blanket down.

Tom rolled over, then bolted upright and skittered clumsily to the side.

"You don't *really* want to block out the sounds of joy," Charlie said, repeating Tom's thoughts back to him. He was sitting on the edge of Tom's bed, in his uniform. Looking right at him.

"What're you doing?" It was all Tom could think to say.

"I opened my gift," Charlie confessed, holding up his glove. "I know we always waited until Christmas morning. I hope you don't mind my cheating a little."

Tom yipped. But not from fear. "Where did you come from?" he managed. And then regretted asking. What if it made Charlie disappear? He felt so solid sitting there on Tom's bed—his legs even pushed the edge of the mattress down—and yet, he also seemed a little like smoke trapped in a jar. Loosen the lid and all in a single *woosh*, he'd slip away, dissipate.

"Would you believe me if I told you I'm from the Land of Second Chances?"

Tom just panted, unsure of everything.

"Would you believe me if I told you I wanted to give Maxwell Ross a second chance—but in the end, it doesn't appear I had to give up everything to do that?"

"I don't understand."

"Come on," Charlie said. "A game of catch."

"But Mom. And I'm in my pajamas," Tom protested.

"Our secret. Get your coat."

They went outside, into the front yard, beneath the giant oak. Tom in his pajamas and his boots and his stocking cap, Charlie in his uniform only. Short sleeves. Not that the cold seemed to bother him.

"Here," Charlie said, motioning for Tom to come closer. He buttoned the top button on the boy's wool Monarch coat, the one he wore to school every day. And he grabbed both ends of the red muffler Tom's mother had knitted, cinching it tight. "Can't have you catching a cold on Christmas."

Tom didn't want his dad to let go. He smelled like himself—like aftershave and Lucky Strikes. He didn't want his dad to be backing up, like he was, widening a giant gap between them. He didn't want him to go, even if it was only to the other side of the yard, and even if the gap only allowed them to have themselves a catch. He wanted to wrap his arms around Charlie's neck, tell him how much he'd missed him.

But Charlie, he also knew, would have none of it. No sentimental schmaltz.

With the first smack of the ball in Charlie's palm, he smiled, shook his head. "Great glove, Tommy," he said with admiration. "Just perfect."

They tossed the ball there, under the moonlight. The neighborhood was silent, but buzzing with all the hopes that everyone had taken to bed with them—the dreams of what tomorrow morning would bring.

And then, one last catch by Charlie. He turned the ball over in his hand a moment, digging a thumb into the stitching.

"Tommy," he said. "Listen. I didn't just come for the catch. I came to tell you something."

"What?"

Charlie thought a moment. Said, "I can give out second chances. Still."

"What are you talking about?"

"I'm still around," Charlie said. "And I can give second chances. Grant wishes. But not for any old thing. Okay? It has to be for something good and important. Not—for a grade, or for a girl, even. Something life-changing. When things are looking like they'll never get any better, or have come to an end. When it looks like your life story's going to end up a tragedy, I have the power to turn everything around. Like I said, though, it can't be for small stuff. There will be a lot of wishes in your life that you'll make that will go unanswered, because I don't have any power over those. But don't lose faith, okay? No matter how many times your wishes go ignored. Don't think it's never going to happen. Promise?"

And then, Tommy's eyes opened.

He was in bed, the pillow beneath him a little sweaty.

He rolled over, the earliest streaks of sunlight coming through his window. It was Christmas.

And he'd had a dream.

A lovely dream.

And maybe, he thought, that dream of his was really a kind of Christmas present in itself. Maybe it was by far the best thing he'd get that day.

It made the prospect of having to open the presents from his father sting a little less, anyway.

He pulled himself from bed, tied on his robe. He would put the percolator on the stove, snag the paper from the front step. He could do that for his mother. She hadn't had a lovely dream. Surely not one as good as his.

What a nice idea, he thought as he unlocked the front door. *Dad looking over me, prepared to grant me my deepest, most important wish.*

Yes, what a lovely little fantasy. As good as any Christmas story ever told.

Stepping onto the front porch, he found that the dream he'd had about Charlie had made the world look a bit different. The snow sparkled brighter. Chimney smoke smelled better—almost like the Lucky Strike scent he'd imagined in his father's uniform. Life didn't seem quite so harsh or quite as full of dead ends as he reached down to pick the paper up off the front step.

As he was turning around, his eyes landed on the porch railing.

A baseball glove was perched on top of it.

Tom stared at the glove. Took a step toward it. Another. Slowly, cautiously, he reached for it. As soon as his fingers touched the thick, new leather, he knew it was the same glove Wolferman had sold him.

A card tumbled out of the palm. Tom squatted, and had to try twice to pick it up, his hand was trembling so badly. Tom's name had been written across the envelope. No return address.

As his shuddering breath made snowballs in the morning air, Tom flipped the back flap of the envelope.

The card inside had a giant green tree on the cover. And a bright red cursive "Merry Christmas" above it.

Inside, a familiar script read, "Thanks for the catch."

15.

Elizabeth watched as Tom picked up his wine glass, took another sip.

"And?" she insisted.

"And, I had Christmas. A great one."

"Oh, come on. You know what I mean."

"I told everyone. Of course I did. Shouted it from the rooftops. I thought I'd experienced a Christmas miracle. I had the Christmas card from Dad as proof! Everyone else thought Mom had written that card for me. As a way to help me through such a hard time."

"What did your mother say?"

"I never asked her."

"Never?" Helen asked.

"I couldn't have stood it, to look into her face and see even the slightest hint that it could be true. That she had written that card."

Tom chuckled, pointing at Elizabeth's plate. "If you scrape that fork any harder, you're going to actually dig into Helen's china."

Elizabeth's face flamed.

"Get you another serving?" Helen asked.

"I would love another serving," Elizabeth confessed.

Helen beamed as she gathered Elizabeth's plate and headed back to her stove. She hummed, the knives and spoons and baking pan turning into a percussion section.

"Where'd you learn to cook like that?" Elizabeth asked.

"This is my own personal instructor," Helen admitted, carrying a cookbook to the table along with Elizabeth's second helping. "I got it for Christmas one year. First Christmas after I got married. Been with me ever since."

"Sounds like it's a bit of a story," Elizabeth said.

"It's my life," Helen said, patting the cover, "right here in these pages."

Elizabeth flipped through it, reading the notes. All the dates in the margins. "Christmas '85" next to the duck, "Hank's birthday '58" next to the prime rib. "Tom's summer barbecue" next to the shish kebabs.

Seeing Tom's name in the cookbook did something to Elizabeth. But then again, the night had already been doing something to Elizabeth. The mention of an old summer barbecue combined with the nearness of his house and the tale he'd shared from boyhood allowed his entire life suddenly to appear, right there in front of her.

And maybe, when she'd told him about the ring, her life had appeared before him, too. Sometimes, the contrast—little you versus grown you, struggling you versus a bustling dress shop owner—offered far more than a single image, a slice of time, ever could.

It was true for Elizabeth, anyway. She felt she understood something about Tom—this older Tom, sitting across from her—that she hadn't before the night had started. He seemed suddenly more three-dimensional. Not just a handsome man in a uniform. Now, she knew he was a man who'd always carried this love for his own father—a kind of unfinished love, really. And knowing it made her replay all the interactions she'd had with Tom in her head, almost like one of Helen's compilation records: the way he'd talked about Geena, the way he'd been with Angela. The proud way of a protective man. His whole life, maybe, was built around this desire to protect—his daughter, his job, all an attempt to soothe the little boy in him who still wished he'd somehow been able to save his own father.

"Did it ever happen?" Elizabeth asked.

"Did what happen?" Tom asked, waving off the offer for a second helping from Helen. "I know there's dessert here somewhere," he told her. "Can't get too full—"

"Your wish," Elizabeth interrupted. "Did you ever get it?"

"Not yet," Tom admitted. "Haven't given up, though."

He nodded once toward the purse Elizabeth had slung over her chair. "Go on," he said. "See what I found for you."

Elizabeth was sure to slide the bite off her fork first. Still chewing, she twisted around, unzipped her bag, and pulled out the piece of paper.

"What is this?" she asked, even though his discovery was written down, right there in front of her.

"The woman's name. The one who started the jewelry company."

He'd written it above a newspaper article from 1933.

"Took a bit of digging in our library," Tom admitted.

Elizabeth held the page. Unable to swallow. Or blink.

"Have you ever met the head librarian?" Tom went on. "She's such a tiny thing. So skinny. Every time I see her—" He stopped mid-sentence. "What is it?" he asked.

"This picture. This woman."

"Yes?"

"I've seen her before. The woman who gave me the ring. The woman who came asking for food at my back door. The woman I keep seeing. This is *her*."

Tom's face drooped. "It can't be."

"Why not?" Helen asked, even though she had not been privy to any of the other details of Elizabeth's story.

"Because," Elizabeth said, "according to this, she died in 1932. Six years before I met her."

16.

Only in Sullivan could the town's one and only librarian be called away from her current read and her living room fire in order to facilitate a late-night emergency need for reference materials.

Then again, she also knew who the request was coming from. And curiosity had made her fire feel suddenly less-than-appealing.

"Thanks, Irene," Tom said as the librarian shuffled up to the door to unlock the entrance. "We owe you."

"What could this place possibly offer you this time of night?" Irene asked, slowly aiming a key for the door. She was an older woman, with a perfectly coiled white bun and the kind of slightly stooped shoulders one got from too many decades spent curled over a book.

She really was thin, Elizabeth thought—as Tom had said earlier. She reminded Elizabeth of a bookmark. Something that had been squashed flat by a heavy object.

"Can't imagine what you'd need in here this time

of night," Irene went on, fishing for an explanation. "I suppose it might be something for a cold case?"

Her eyes twinkled like falling snow. Hoping for something far juicier than the usual town gossip, Elizabeth supposed.

"We need to poke around in your genealogical records," Tom said.

"*Really* cold case," Irene muttered, unlocking the entrance and letting them in.

At that late hour, the library seemed itself a kind of cemetery. It was a feeling that wouldn't let up, not even when Irene flicked on the lights in the local history room.

"Help you two find what you need?"

"We're looking for information on an R. R. Race," Tom said. "She lived in Sullivan at one point, and her jewelry designs were somewhat famous in her time. My research tells me she died in 1932, but Elizabeth here says that can't be true."

"I got out of a cozy chair and ripped myself from my book for this?" Irene asked.

"It's got a good story attached to it," Elizabeth assured her. "Maybe even as good as your book. To start with, I met this woman in 1938."

"Well, now, I really am intrigued." Irene shuffled toward the shelves in the back.

***

"1932," Irene said an hour later, pointing at an article. The fourth, now, to confirm it. R. R. Race, jewelry designer, passed away in February of that year.

Irene put her hands on both sides of the immense volume and twisted it toward the two of them so that they could see it for themselves. In Sullivan, old newspapers were archived in giant volumes—bound books the size of an actual unfolded newspaper—to preserve the original layout and feel of the pages as much as the information they contained.

"But no burial records, no death notice," Tom reminded her.

"Could still be it wasn't '32," Irene said with a shrug, sticking her bottom lip out. "That's how those things went."

"What things?" Elizabeth pressed. At this point, they were surrounded by six paper cups of coffee, all from the hallway vending machine.

"It was hard times," Irene admitted. "The Depression and all. According to this, your R. R. Race's company really started to flounder after Black Tuesday. She had a bunch of layoffs and unpaid vendors. She *disappeared* in '32. That's what these articles say, if you really pay attention. Disappeared. Maybe the family needed her to be more than missing. Maybe they needed to declare her legally dead so they could gain control of the company and try to bring it back to life."

"Maybe," Tom mused.

"Didn't work, if that was the plan," Elizabeth grumbled.

"Doesn't seem that the company was the same without her," Irene agreed.

"And then again, maybe she really did die in '32," Elizabeth said, looking at Tom. "Maybe what I have in that bank is not so unlike that glove of yours."

"Maybe," Tom said, only partially sidestepping the story of the Christmas dream of Charlie, "you don't want to believe your mom wrote you a Christmas card."

"Metaphorically speaking."

"Right."

Irene shook her head. "I'm not following."

"What we mean is," Elizabeth announced, slamming the volume shut, "we want to take you out. Get your coat."

"No good deed goes unpunished?" Irene asked.

"Something like that," Tom told her.

They walked her to Tom's car, where they insisted on Irene sitting between them, in the middle of the bench seat in Tom's Buick.

They sang Christmas carols, their headlights shining all the way. Elizabeth thought of stopping by Tom's neighborhood to pick up Helen as thank-you for the dinner, but by that point, Helen had probably turned in for the night—if not asleep then close to it.

Their breath painted frothy banks of steam on the windshield. And still, they sang. All the way to Ruby's glowing red neon sign.

"I haven't been to Ruby's since my husband died," Irene admitted.

"Well, this'll be a treat," Elizabeth said. "For us, too."

They ushered her out of the Buick, each one of them grasping a hand to make sure she didn't take a tumble on the slippery sidewalk. Tom pushed the green door, and Irene gasped. "Oh, it's exactly like I remembered. If only Bill could see it."

"Irene?" Evie called out, her sequin jacket sparkling as she waved from the piano bench.

Irene waved back, throwing her coat over a nearby chair. "Do you still take requests?" she asked Evie. Her flats scraped on the floor as she rushed to the piano. Evie was already scooting to the side, making room on her bench.

Ruby stopped wiping the bar down to stare at Elizabeth and Tom.

Elizabeth smiled, shrugged.

"You two are gonna be the talk of the town tomorrow," Ruby warned.

As if to agree, Irene and Evie broke into a rousing rendition of "Yes Sir, That's My Baby."

"Whatever's on tap," Tom said, ignoring the musical tease being pounded out on the ivories.

"Two," Elizabeth said.

"That's different," Ruby said.

"Not *that* different," Elizabeth scolded. She knew Ruby didn't just mean the drink—especially since she was looking at Tom when she said it.

***

Tom and Elizabeth dropped Irene off at the library, where Tom helped her into her car.

"I feel bad keeping you out so late," he apologized.

"Don't you dare. I haven't had a night this lovely in ages," Irene said, patting his arm. "The singing! The cocoa! The marshmallows." She clasped her hands in front of her chest. "There's life left in the old gal yet."

"Follow you home?" Tom asked.

"Don't you dare," Irene said again. "I won't be alone. I'll be driving with all my memories. It's a good time of year to do that."

"Yeah," Tom agreed, his nose quickly going pink and his breath making a long steady white stream. "It is."

He and Elizabeth watched her drive off. Her tail-lights flickered red a moment as she pumped her brakes once before rolling off into the cold moonlight.

Tom smiled at Elizabeth. "Not exactly what you had in mind before I picked you up tonight, I'm sure."

"It was so much better."

"Yeah?"

"Yeah."

He stared at her. It was one of those long looks, the kind that asked for permission.

"Take a chance," he whispered—the phrase engraved on her ring.

His head started to lean in toward her, there in the parking lot of the library.

"Even if it's on the middleman," she murmured, tilting her head toward his.

"Come again?" he asked, jerking backward.

Elizabeth coughed. She felt as though she'd been pelted with an ice-packed snowball. "That's me. The middleman. The intermediary. The go-between."

"What does that even mean?"

Elizabeth was shocked at how upset he seemed. "The ring. The woman who made it did something great—she was a jewelry designer. And then I got it, and I've been in charge of it, keeping it safe, until I figure out who to give it to. So that someone else can use it to do something great."

He took another step back. "*What?*"

"That's the only thing that makes sense. A few days ago, I was still imagining the ways I'd use the ring to spend on myself, but I realize now that isn't right. Especially after looking up the designer. It's all finally become clear tonight. I didn't do anything. I borrowed from it. Used the ring as collateral. I opened a dress store. I didn't exactly cure cancer. It's whoever the next person is that will be important. My duty to the ring is to find the next owner."

"That's really what you think?"

"That's what it is."

"You don't think you did anything."

"Pfff," Elizabeth said, offering a dismissive toss of the hand.

Tom opened the passenger side door. Silently, he drove her home.

He idled in the driveway, clearly intent on not walking her to the door.

Elizabeth squirmed, feeling like she'd done something wrong.

"We're going to Ruby's on Christmas Eve," Tom announced, staring through the windshield.

"I always go with my niece. It's our night."

Tom whipped his head around to look at her.

"It's our tradition," she tried again.

"I'm going to be there," he said. "Christmas Eve.

Find me."

"Why don't we go another night—"

"No," Tom said. "It has to be Christmas Eve."

17.

The air was smelling more and more like Christmas—or so Elizabeth thought after dropping a new dress off at Irene's a few mornings later. A Christmas Eve dress, perfect for another visit to Ruby's Place. It wasn't just the snow or the pine; there was a smell to anticipation, Elizabeth had always thought. As the calendar crept still closer and closer, she could smell it. As strong and unmistakable as the smell of a fresh pot of coffee.

Though Irene protested, saying her years at Ruby's had come and gone, she'd accepted the dress—and Elizabeth was certain that she smelled it on her, too. One distinct whiff of anticipation as she turned and shut the door.

Pleased with herself, Elizabeth had returned to her car and headed back to her store, this time to officially start the day.

It was clear, as Elizabeth approached the square,

that Sullivan had exploded in its usual pre-Christmas frenzy. To be sure, as soon as the Thanksgiving dishes were scraped, store traffic instantly picked up. But now? Not a single available parking space could be found around the square. The 25% Off signs had come down from every single store, replaced by 50% Off, or 2-For-1. It had never quite seemed right to Elizabeth to essentially punish those who'd come first to get all their shopping done. So the sign Elizabeth had instructed her girls to hang that morning offered: *75% Off w/ Receipt for Any Previous December Purchase.*

Elizabeth steered her enormous Lincoln through the square, envious of the shoppers with their lists. The gifts that had already been decided on. She was even more envious of the shoppers who had set out without a clue, who'd simply trusted they'd know the right gift when they saw it.

Funny—Elizabeth *had* a gift. The greatest gift of all time. It was just that she had no idea who to give it to. (And despite Tom's reaction the night before, she was still certain that was the right thing to do. To find the next owner.)

She also knew, as she continued to drive, was that her ring *should* have gone to Angela. Logically speaking, anyway. Elizabeth was what the outside world had officially deemed an old woman. Even if she didn't like the label, there was no denying there would never be a child at this point—Angela was as close as she'd ever get.

And yet…

Elizabeth was already giving so much to Angela. She'd drawn up the will to give her (or, really, her parents)

138

her estate. At the end, when the credits were rolling on her life, everything Elizabeth owned—her home and her accounts and her store—would go to her sister's family, and then trickle down to Angela.

But somehow, that didn't seem to be keeping with the spirit of the ring. What the stranger had done in the kitchen of Elizabeth's youth had been the epitome of grand gestures. Elizabeth felt it was her responsibility to do something grand with it now. Lawyers and estates and relatives weren't grand. Doing what was logical wasn't grand.

The horrible part was, Elizabeth could have already been doing something grand. She'd been sitting on a regular fortune. And what had she done? Put it away in a locked box in Walter's bank. The ring hadn't even been seen in all that time, which seemed a travesty.

When she thought of the way Tom had pulled away from her the night before, shaken his head with disdain at her regret—and her need to find the right person for its next owner—her whole body started heating up. She was kind of mad at Tom, frankly. What had she said that wasn't painfully obvious?

To spite him, she imagined skipping Ruby's on Christmas. Or staying away long enough for the crowds to have all gone, then knocking on the front window as Ruby was closing up shop.

"What's with you, kid?" Ruby would grumble, but Elizabeth would tell her, "I come bearing two hands ready to help you close—and your Christmas gift." And the two of them would open a bottle of champagne and put on the radio and they would dance as they mopped the floor.

The two rarely gave each other gifts, but that year, Elizabeth would give Ruby a—

—a what?

That ring was messing with her. Doing strange things to her mind. Usually, Elizabeth had no trouble coming up with a gift idea. She figured that part of her brain—the giving part, the part that could match inanimate objects to people, the part that knew what would bring a flush to the cheeks or a gasp bursting out from behind a pair of lips—got a workout every day. Every customer who stepped in her store offered Elizabeth yet another opportunity to figure out the perfect dress for the woman in front of her, not to mention the perfect shoes or purse or pin to go with it. Now, though, that part of her head used for matching people with things seemed to be limping along. Why couldn't she figure this out? She'd even returned to the bank for another look, hoping that seeing the ring would have sparked something. Hoping that gemstone would talk to her, tell her what to do.

And still, she had nothing. Maybe, she thought, she hadn't yet met the right person for the ring.

Which also seemed ludicrous.

Her mind went back to Angela, the real reason she couldn't avoid Tom on Christmas Eve. The reason she couldn't show up at Ruby's closing, like she'd just fantasized. Sweet Angela counted on their Christmas Eves together.

They wouldn't last forever, the Christmas Eves. Elizabeth knew that. It wouldn't be long before Angela was going to want fast lanes and the company of other young people. The time to enjoy Angela was now, before

Angela turned her attention to something flashier, louder. Soon, Elizabeth would become an antique in Angela's mind, something quaint and pretty but with no real purpose.

That was life.

Most things faded.

Everything except that *ring*.

What Tom wanted to talk to her about on Christmas Eve—was it the ring? Did he have some idea about what she should do with it? She hoped not.

"He might not show," she tried to console herself, but somehow, she knew that wasn't true. Tom had something else to say to her. He would be there.

The idea of that gave her pangs of dread and anticipation all at the same time. She had so enjoyed their evening out together. Maybe she never should have told him about the ring at all.

As Elizabeth edged the front bumper ever closer to her usual space beyond Rossi's entrance, she began to wonder if she hadn't overshot a bit with that sign of hers. The line to Rossi's stretched from her front door all the way down the street, blocking the entrances to some of her neighbors' shops—the stationery store and the men's suit shop appeared to be getting the worst of it.

She might have felt guilty if she had not known the entire line was window shopping as they waited to get inside her store, jotting down in their minds what they'd be back to buy after visiting Rossi's.

Down the street, Roy Weber stood outside his electronics store, puffing away on one of his Pall Malls. Disgusted at her success and clearly blaming her entirely for the traffic jams.

Elizabeth smiled at him as she pulled herself from her car, trying on a friendly but unsuccessful wave. And then she turned her smile to her customers. "Hello, ladies," she rang out as she unlocked her entrance. The shoppers gushed in while the faces of the models and the cashiers twisted into wide-eyed alarm. As Elizabeth passed one salesgirl, she could have sworn she heard her chanting, "End-of-year commission" like a refrain to get her through the day.

By three o'clock that afternoon, everything in Rossi's looked limp: the last few remaining designer blouses on hangers, the strings of white lights, even the store models, some of whom had stolen seats in the break room, their heads on a table that had been used for gift wrapping. When Elizabeth came stomping in to check on them, Gertie (a seasonal hire there to earn enough money for her new husband's Christmas gift) raised up, a silver bow plastered to her left eyebrow.

Elizabeth laughed as she tossed her hand, beckoning them all back onto the sales floor.

They were all shocked to see her turn the Closed sign to the street.

"We've got three more hours," Millicent said, checking her watch.

"Not today," Elizabeth insisted. "Great as the final tally must be, this one's been rough on everyone." She offered a reassuring tilt of her head, announcing, "We're going to straighten up, get today's delivery out of the back, and set the floor up for tomorrow. And then everyone's going home, to rest up. Only three more days till Christmas. At this rate, we'll have to haul the clothes out of my closet to give the good people of Sullivan something to buy." She smiled at the image—an empty closet that she would have to fill with all new things. *What torture*, she thought to herself sarcastically.

The promise of going home perked her girls up, helped them find the energy for a sprint to unbox and hang and straighten. Once coats were gathered, Elizabeth raced to beat them to the door, slipping hundred-dollar bills into their hands as they left—the models and the cashiers and even the part-time dressing room help who blinked in disbelief.

"Hey, Millicent," Elizabeth called out, grabbing onto her arm before she could gather her purse and coat, "is that a new lock on the register?"

Millicent glanced over her shoulder. "Oh. Yeah. I should have told you. It got so busy—anyway, that kid was here again."

"Michael?"

"Right. He was here this morning. Before you got here, even. Fixed up all the register drawers. He said that was part of his deal with you."

"It is." Actually, Michael was early. It wasn't the weekend yet.

"Well, he said he wanted to know if that settled his debt. How did he put it exactly? He wanted to know if he was no longer on probation." Millicent chuckled. "He did the front alarm, just like the back. He wanted me to ask you if you needed anything else. He said something about you knowing how to get in touch with him."

"Yeah," Elizabeth said. "Thanks, Millicent." Instead of the hundred, Elizabeth slipped her a far-more-than-expected bonus check.

"This is too—"

"Oh, pfff. It is not. Take it or I'll be offended. I wanted all you girls to have your money when there was still a little time left. Time to buy Christmas dinner, at least."

Millicent hugged her—but not because of the money. "You're good for that kid, you know."

"Please." But it was a thought that warmed Elizabeth just the same.

It was still early in the day when Elizabeth left the store. But her feet and her muscles were screaming out for rest. Begging. She was too tired to even feel hungry.

Leaving the square, she saw her. Again. The woman in the black cloak. Walking down the sidewalk, near the driver's side of her Lincoln.

Elizabeth gasped. She scrambled to roll her window down. "Excuse me," she called. "Hello?"

The woman ignored her.

"Ma'am?" Elizabeth called. "Ma'am!"

When that didn't work, she honked her horn twice—two short beeps.

The woman didn't flinch. Or so much as glance her way.

Instead, she disappeared down an alley between a shoe repair shop and an old medical clinic.

Without thinking about the consequences, Elizabeth pulled into the No Parking zone near the alley. She thrust her body out from the driver's seat and ran to catch up, desperate to speak to whoever she was. R. R. Race?

It couldn't be.

But then again—who else could it be?

"Excuse me," Elizabeth tried again. "Wait. We need to talk." She wanted so desperately for the date Tom found to be wrong. The designer of the ring couldn't have died in 1932. She wanted Irene's explanation to be closer to the truth—that this woman was one of many wayward souls who had hit bottom and then simply found another life elsewhere during the Depression.

The articles had all said the woman was from Sullivan. Couldn't she have come back? Couldn't she be here now, an old woman, retired? Couldn't she be stepping back into Elizabeth's line of sight—over and over—because she wanted to see what Elizabeth had done with her gift? Or because she had another message for her? Or wanted it back?

"Ma'am?" Elizabeth called, her voice echoing against the brick walls in the alley.

The woman opened a door facing the alley and stepped inside.

Elizabeth lunged, grabbing onto the door before it could fall shut.

Yet again, the woman was nowhere to be seen. The hallway was empty.

Until a familiar silhouette stepped into the faint light.

"Michael," Elizabeth said.

He turned, his body slumping with disappointment the moment he saw her. "I already came by your place."

"I know—Millicent said. Didn't you have school?"

"Got canceled. Some sort of emergency teachers' meeting or...something. I wanted to get done at your place early so I could come here."

"But what is here?"

He shrugged. "An old-folks' place."

"Do you have someone who needs to be cared for? Did you come to visit someone?"

He shrugged again. "No."

Elizabeth sighed with exasperation. "Michael. Please."

"Look, I just like to come here."

"An eighteen-year-old boy likes to be around ninety-year-olds."

"Yeah. I fix lots of stuff. More than cash drawers."

"Like what?"

"Motorized wheelchairs sometimes, or carts for oxygen tanks. Sometimes radios or old record players."

Surprise washed over Elizabeth.

"Don't tell anybody."

"Why not?"

"Because—it's something I do, okay? It doesn't need to get out."

Elizabeth wanted to probe. This was by far the most intriguing thing she'd uncovered about Michael Harris. But everyone deserved a little section of life that was all their own, that belonged only to them. And so she let up on her grip.

Instead, she asked, "Did you happen to see a woman come through here? In a black cloak?"

"I haven't seen anybody come in through the back since I got here."

"Weird. Maybe I was mistaken about her coming inside. Maybe she's still in the alley."

When Elizabeth turned toward the back door, Michael caught her arm. "That door locks behind you. You'll have to go out the front."

They walked down the main hall into a large open area. She had to admit it didn't feel much like Christmas inside the facility. Nurse's uniforms were far more prevalent than white twinkling lights and the smell of lemon disinfectant filled the air. The small artificial tree near the entrance, adorned with only a few red glass balls, seemed like little more than an afterthought. She scanned the wrinkled faces, hoping to find a pair of violet eyes.

"How mobile are the residents here?" Elizabeth asked softly.

"Mobile?" he repeated.

"Are they able to get out? Go for walks, that kind of thing?"

"This isn't hospice or anything. They just need some daily help. There's still plenty of dancing that goes on in this joint. Even if there wasn't," he added, as a way of explaining his presence, "everyone should have their favorite music. When I go, I want music playing."

Before she was ready for it, Michael was holding the door for her. She looked back, sadness overtaking her. She wished she hadn't decided to leave Michael's life private. She wanted to pick at it, like one of the gossips who had long tried to get at the truth of her love life.

Instead, she announced, "You're coming back. Friday. To my store."

He let out a grunt of frustration. A frown buckled

his face as he threw his weight onto one leg in a disappointed slouch. "But I did everything you asked."

"Yes, but you still have my friend's dolly. We have to return it."

His face started to turn pink. "I didn't mean—I wasn't trying to steal it."

"Oh, I know," Elizabeth said. "I'm not accusing. But there's unfinished business. Don't come so early, though. Come in the afternoon."

He was already trying to back up, slink away from her when she called, "Bring your amp."

***

The "unfinished" part, of course, had to do with far more than a dolly.

Michael arrived that Friday afternoon, so close to three o'clock that Elizabeth wondered, for a split second, if he'd actually gone to school that day. She remembered lingering at lockers when she was his age, taking plenty of time to flirt or detour on the way home for an ice cream soda.

Not Michael, though.

He rattled the dolly through the door, snagging the attention of the customers pushing hangers about on racks.

"I was about to take this straight to Ruby, but I didn't know if you wanted me to stop here first."

"Where's your amp?" Elizabeth asked.

"In—my car."

"Get it," she ordered.

Michael sighed, dragging the dolly behind him. He had a rough time getting it out Rossi's front door—it banged and clattered against the glass, the door insisting on shutting while he was still trying to get out.

Elizabeth would have tried to help, but she was gathering her own purchase from behind the front counter. One she'd made earlier that day, from Hoover's Music, while on break.

From the counter, Millicent threw a startled look at Elizabeth.

"Oh, pfff," Elizabeth said with a toss of her hand. And then she was out the door, too.

Michael stood on the sidewalk, one hand in his coat pocket, the other wrapped around the handle of the dolly that was tilted backward and ready to roll. His face looked a little tortured, but that only made Elizabeth race down the sidewalk quicker.

Behind her, the dolly rattled and banged as Michael fought to keep up.

Elizabeth opened the bright green Ruby's Place door and ushered him inside with a slight bow and a flourish of her arm. Unamused, Michael dragged himself inside.

"There it is!" Ruby shouted, pointing at her dolly. "I was beginning to wonder, you two."

"We have a proposition," Elizabeth said.

"What's that, kid?"

"I have no idea," Michael answered.

"Hush—she was talking to me," Elizabeth told him.

She looked back at the piano. But the bench was

empty.

"Where's Evie? Doesn't she usually come to plan out her Christmas playlist a couple of days early? Get all her holiday sheet music ready?"

"She took a break," Ruby said, pointing toward the restroom. "Why?"

But instead of answering, Elizabeth tugged on Michael's arm. "Come on. Hurry," she said, racing toward the piano.

"Plug it in," she said, while pulling a microphone and a stand from her Hoover's Music shopping bag. She was still trying to figure out the telescoping stand and how best to place it near the piano's soundboard when Evie returned, bellowing, "What's the big idea?"

"Oh, now you're going to get it," Ruby called from the front of the room. "Nobody messes with Evie's ivories."

"We wanted to show you something," Elizabeth said.

"We?" Evie echoed.

"How many years have you played Christmas Eve here?"

"Too many to count."

"And how many years have you had so many people join in on the carols that your piano was completely drowned out?"

"An equal number."

"What if you could play and be heard this year?" Elizabeth asked, pointing to Michael's amp.

"I never have used a mic," Evie said, squatting to get a look.

Michael immediately launched into the sales pitch he'd memorized for Roy Weber. As he talked, he fiddled with the dials, showing Evie how it worked.

"What brought this on?" Ruby asked in her ear.

Elizabeth jumped, shocked to find Ruby standing at her side.

"Everyone should have their music," Elizabeth said, echoing what Michael had told her at the nursing home.

When he raised his head, Michael was smiling at her.

18.

Sullivan, December 24. Christmas Eve.

At a quarter to five, Elizabeth and her girls were still ringing up the stragglers. Even the store's piped-in carols sounded out of breath and a little whiny—like they, too, were dying to take off their shoes.

"This place looks like the Whos' houses after the Grinch got through with them," Millicent remarked, glancing about the store.

Elizabeth laughed—a weary, creaky kind of laugh—but it was true: discount displays and circular racks were largely empty, the pyramids of costume jewelry picked-over (only a few stray boxes remained). The last of the sweaters clung to hangers by one shoulder, while a few skirts (mostly those found to be defective in some way from all the handling, now featuring hanging threads or broken zippers) dangled at a crooked slant. Holiday garlands clung to their spots with the last shred of strength they had, ready to tumble to the floor.

Even the mannequins looked like they were begging to sit down.

Elizabeth and her girls straightened up as best they could, settled cash drawers, and locked up.

"We all need to be here bright and early on the twenty-sixth for a floor change," Elizabeth reminded them. It was her usual schedule: the store would be completely empty on Christmas Day. The day after, it was closed to the public, giving Elizabeth and her girls time to take down the decorations, put up new displays. Highlight dresses for Valentine's Day, put out the last of the stylish coats or hats or boots to get through what was often the worst part of winter in Missouri—the weeks immediately following Christmas. Elizabeth often started talking to her girls about plans for the spring and summer seasons. Always looking ahead.

"In the meantime, though, the Christmas season at Rossi's is officially over!" Elizabeth announced. The girls cheered and applauded one another. Elizabeth stood at the door, where she thanked each of her girls individually, passed out presents—tiny wrapped boxes with a little something special inside—and kissed everyone on the cheek as they left. It was enough to put the sparkle back in them.

Now, it was time for them all to hurry home—to change into the outfits they had long ago picked out, saved up for, even purchased on layaway if they happened to be on the extravagantly expensive side. Slip into silk stockings and cashmere sweaters. Pull out grandmother's pearls and fasten the straps of high heels around their ankles.

Elizabeth raced, too. She put on the dress she'd special ordered for herself, set aside for this very occasion: a red V-neck ankle-length jersey dress, adorned with silver streaks of interwoven stitches over the shoulders and around the large bell sleeves. Silver earrings and silver pumps completed the outfit. Then, of course, came the crowning touches: the perfect chignon, nail polish and lipstick a perfect match for the shade of her dress, and a puff of her signature Cashmere Bouquet powder.

She slipped into her winter white angora topcoat, grabbed the keys to Oscar, and was out the door, on her way to Angela's house.

Angela burst through her front door before Elizabeth could even finish pulling into the drive.

Her mother's voice could be heard calling out to her, but it was no use. Elizabeth was on her way to Christmas Eve at Ruby's with Aunt Elizabeth. A night of sparkling and magic.

Angela twittered in the seat as Elizabeth drove. And when she finally pulled into the lot, Angela was the first out of the car.

She raced to Ruby's front door, like a child racing to a swimming pool or an amusement park. But then again, all of Sullivan raced to Ruby's on Christmas. It had been that way for more than twenty years.

It was where you went to be seen, after all.

It was where you went to celebrate.

It was where you went for the best meal of your life.

And, Elizabeth was reminded as she opened the door, it was where you went to sing.

The entire room swelled with voices. All of them belting out "Here We Come a-Wassailing" as though it were a drinking song. Arms around shoulders all through the room—making an unending human chain. They swayed back and forth. A few men raised beer mugs. Kids were propped on shoulders.

They were together. One big joyous bunch.

It was beautiful. But then, it was beautiful every year.

Elizabeth took a moment to look the place over—Ruby really had outdone herself. The garland was thicker and greener and more fragrant. The candles softer, casting flickering shadows. The air smelled of her usual prime rib dinner, though it appeared she was also offering a duck option. Wafts of cocoa came floating through on occasion, smelling even richer than usual. Ruby'd also devised an entire new menu of mixed drinks, which was hanging on the wall behind the bar. She'd hung a few framed black and whites throughout the place—that was a new shot of Dorothy, the original singer, Elizabeth noted, near the tinsel-wrapped mirror behind the bar. That shot of her in her cloche hat and charmeuse gown made it easy to believe the old Sullivan rumors were true, that the jazz singer really had performed in the building when it was a speakeasy.

But the image that garnered the most attention was the giant picture of Ida—what appeared to be a professional headshot, there with her youthful face and her hair piled up on top of her head, her high-necked dress offering a white ruffle under her dark chin.

"Really great this year, Ruby," Elizabeth could hear

one of the patrons shout.

"It's all for her," Ruby shouted back, pointing at Ida's image.

Ruby'd put up a Christmas tree in every single corner, too, fully decorated. Another stood behind the piano. She'd apparently stuffed presents under those trees, because several men (decked out in red felt Santa hats, no less) were passing them out, tossing them into the crowd. The boxes were then bounced off fingertips like volleyballs, passed from one patron to another, toward the final landing spot: whoever had just entered the bar.

"Hey!" Ruby warned. "Some of that stuff needs a gentle touch, now."

"Okay, okay." It was Walter who said it, dressed that night in his very best suit, a dark gray three-piece with a red and green plaid tie. He snagged a box and raced it over to Elizabeth.

Elizabeth only stared him down.

"Gotcha," Walter said, redirecting himself. "Angie!" he called out to Elizabeth's niece.

Elizabeth hung up her coat, then set about twisting her way through the crowd, knowing she would find Angela at the bar.

No matter how busy it got on Christmas Eve, Angela could always find a spot there, almost as though an invisible hand had saved a stool for her. Her very own island where she could eat and watch—and learn how the grown-ups acted the night before Christmas. Maybe even pretend to be a little grown-up herself.

Ruby had already served up a helping of her homemade cocoa and marshmallows. And Angela was already attacking those marshmallows with a spoon, digging into them and gobbling up a giant mouthful. "Haaaah," she moaned, putting the spoon down and waving at her open mouth with her hand.

"You're always too eager," Elizabeth scolded, as Ruby scooted a glass of ice water Angela's way.

"Hey, kid. You're looking especially lovely to-night," Ruby noted. Ruby was herself looking festive in a pair of full black pleated pants and a white silk poet's blouse, picked out by Elizabeth herself. "Wouldn't have anything to do with a certain gentleman caller, would it?"

"Oh, pfff," Elizabeth dismissed with a toss of her hand.

"What is it with all this stuff about Aunt Elizabeth and men?" Angela moaned.

"Oh, you'll have a beau before I do, don't you wor-ry," Elizabeth assured her.

Both Angela and Ruby rolled their eyes, but for different reasons.

Angela downed another couple of bites of her marshmallows before racing off to join the singers, scoot-ing her way through the crowd until she could prop her-self on a corner of Evie's piano bench.

"He's here," Ruby leaned in to say.

Elizabeth turned, and there he was: Tom, sitting to the side of the bar, at a table by himself. Looking hand-some, of course, in his dark suit. The tie was more attrac-tive, but it also wasn't. Elizabeth loved the story attached to the other one, the daughter and the gift and how he would never let her down by changing out of it, even when she was out of sight.

It was a small thing, really, the wearing of an ugly tie. But maybe, Elizabeth also thought, that was where true character could always be found. In the tiny, seemingly unimportant moments. Maybe in the quiet corners, where shadows would keep the truth mostly hidden, maybe how a man decided to act *there* was where he could be seen in his entirety.

"You came," Elizabeth said, getting up to join him.

"I told you I would." Tom stood to pull out the other chair at his table for two.

"No daughter?" Elizabeth asked, sitting at his table.

"Nah. Geena's with her mom and the soon-to-be stepdad tonight."

"That's rough."

"I get Christmas Day."

Elizabeth nodded. He was staring at her. Eyes probing. But why?

"You still feel the same?" he asked.

"About?"

Tom leaned forward. Elizabeth liked the fact that he was leaning forward. "Your ring. The idea that you're nothing but a go-between, that you didn't do anything special."

She shrugged.

"*Look*, Lizzie," he scolded.

"Look at what?"

"Them." Tom pointed. "What do you see?"

Elizabeth took a deep breath. "I see Ruby's Place. I see people celebrating. I see gifts and joy and I see Christmas Eve. I see that Ruby worked even more magic this year than in previous years. I see that giant picture of Ida. I see what a special place this is."

Tom clenched his jaw as she spoke, like her words were giving him a toothache.

"Know what I see?" he asked.

Elizabeth raised her eyebrow, crossing her arms over her chest.

"I see Betty Weber. In what?"

Elizabeth followed his stare. "Pants."

"I bet you sold her those, didn't you?"

"Who else—"

"Where is she?"

"She's sort of table hopping," Elizabeth said, watching her move between the tables where various city council members and their families dined.

"Where is she usually?" Tom asked.

"At a table with Roy." Elizabeth straightened up in her seat, squaring her shoulders as she realized what she'd just said. "She—"

"Right. Look at Betty out there, wearing her pants. Off to table hop on her own this year, not glued to her husband's side. Moving about the bar like *she's* a woman of importance. Like she can make her own decisions.

"Look there, at Joan," Tom went on, "who's been recovering from cancer treatment. How elegant and happy she suddenly is. Almost like, in order to put on those clothes you picked for her, she could take *off* something else. A little worry, maybe. The ache of the unknown.

"Look at Irene," Tom said. "Lost her husband, couldn't stand to come back. But here she is, in the outfit you hand-delivered after our library run."

"How did you know—" Elizabeth started.

"She told me all about that when I stopped by the library to thank her again for opening for us," Tom said.

"She came," Elizabeth said, eyeing her in the silver satin dress with the black and silver woven ankle-length jacket, an outfit made for a queen.

"You can't be surprised," Tom said. "No way would a woman choose not to be seen in *that*."

Elizabeth chuckled; she'd thought something similar picking it out.

"They're all here, and they're not just celebrating," Tom said. "They're different. But why? Because they're here? A building doesn't make a person feel different about themselves, Lizzie. But clothes, now, they make the man. Right?"

Elizabeth stammered. Muttered something incoherent as Tom's words continued to permeate.

"Even Roy," Tom said. "He's come with a woman in a pantsuit. It's forced him to behave more like an open-minded man. So open-minded he's now in the back, talking to Michael. Reversing his decision not to showcase that amp in his electronics store. It's happening, Elizabeth. Change. All those promises we make to ourselves at the end of the year to be better, happier, more successful. It starts right here. But Ruby doesn't do that. Not all of it. I don't even think she does most of it. Clothes make a person feel different. I've known that for a long time, Lizzie. Felt it the first time I put on my own police uniform.

"You *did that*, Liz," he insisted, pointing at the jubilant crowd. "You do it every single year. You do it at your shop now, but you did it before, at Graham's Department Store. You've been dressing the people of Sullivan for Christmas Eve every single year that Ruby's Place has been in business. Yes, there's magic here in this building. But these nights would be a fraction of what they are without your hand in them. That's not a little thing. It's not a middleman kind of thing. It's an important thing. One of the *most* important things."

Elizabeth trembled.

"What is it? You see it, don't you?"

"Yes," she said, her voice only barely audible over the din. "I do." She saw the glitter of the night, the air suddenly swirling like northern lights. She saw the year gone by, every single day of it, the year everyone had spent—the triumphs and the mundane day-to-day all mixed together. The comings and the goings, the mail deliveries and the laundry and the school open houses. The dinners with the boss. The weddings and the births. She saw midnights and mid-mornings, coffee cake and tea. She saw the lives everyone in Sullivan had built around one another. And she saw more; she saw tomorrow; she saw lives that wanted to be bigger, fuller.

It was there, in the cut of the shirt, in the length of the skirt. It tumbled out of pockets. It held together the seams.

Next year, we can be this, but we can be more, too.

In the mirror, in the clothes Elizabeth sold, they could see it. They could see their dreams. And if they could see it, it was real. It was right to believe in it.

Her eyes prickled, a surge of pride swelling.

Because she saw something else, too.

She saw her answer.

19.

The *noise* that year—it was something. Louder than ever. Talking, laughing. Glasses clinking. Still, Evie's piano notes soared. Attacked Elizabeth's ears with the joy of Christmas.

If Elizabeth had made everyone feel a little different—like someone with fewer problems, smaller problems, someone brighter or shinier—by simply dressing them for the night, then Michael had helped to provide a closeness. A sense of camaraderie. That night, the music was fabric. A single piece of cloth that connected them all. Bound them ever tighter together.

"Lizzie!" Tom called out as Elizabeth stood, pushed her chair away from his table, and began to make her way through the crowd. Weaving in and out, in-between bodies, her feet following the rhythm of Michael's music.

"Lizzie!" Tom tried again, elbowing his way between merrymakers. "Where are you going?"

She stopped, scanning the crowd. *Surely he didn't*

leave, she thought. When a couple rose to their feet to dance, Elizabeth attacked one of their chairs, claimed it as her own. She tugged her silver heels free and climbed onto the chair, her stockings making her feet slippery against the hard wooden seat. Now nearly two feet taller than anyone else in the room, she put her hands on her hips and searched through the faces.

A bewildered Angela waved at her from the bar. Elizabeth waved back, as Ruby put her hands on her hips and shook her head.

Finally—there he was. The blond hair, the bare-ly-in-existence mustache. One of the few not dressed up—or, at least, not wearing a suit. Instead, he had on a pair of cords and a flannel shirt. And he was drinking one of Ruby's cocoas in the small space between the piano and the wall, near the amp he had built.

Elizabeth scurried down, ducked, zigged between the last of the thick clump of carolers standing between her and the piano.

"Michael!" she called.

"Lizzie!" Tom shouted.

Michael frowned. "What—?" he started, but Elizabeth grabbed his arm. "You're coming with me," she said. With Tom on her heels, she dragged Michael over to Walter, still pulling presents out from under one of Ruby's trees.

"We have to go. Now," Elizabeth told him.

"Where?" He pulled himself away from the tree, rising up so quickly, it disturbed his Santa hat, sent it tumbling down over his eyebrows. With both of his hands still full of presents, Walter used the back of his wrist to push the hat out of his eye.

"To the bank," Elizabeth said.

"Now?" Walter asked. "I'm here with my son."

Scott was right beside him, trying to look grown-up in his own three-piece blue surge suit. But he was having far too good of a time in his own Santa hat, handing out presents, to look anywhere close to debonair—as he'd surely imagined he would as he'd dressed for the night. Something about childish giddiness kept a person from looking smooth and polished.

"He'll be fine here on his own for a little while. Send him over to sing with Angela," Elizabeth said, wrapping her hand around Walter's wrist.

"What's going on? What do we have to do now that we can't do after Christmas? What's so urgent?" Walter asked.

"I think this idea has been festering all along," Elizabeth said. "I finally just recognize it."

The four of them—Elizabeth and Michael and Walter and Tom—all walked to the bank. It was only a block away, but it was torture for Elizabeth. Her legs moved through sludge. Why wasn't anyone else as anxious as she was? Why didn't they suspect that she hadn't asked Walter to give up being Santa and distributing gifts, but that she was roping him into helping her give the biggest gift of all?

At the entrance of the bank, they stood on the sidewalk while Walter fished for his keys. Elizabeth's lungs burned, begging for oxygen. But it was so hard to do anything at all—even inhale—before she got this done. This job that had been given to her so long ago.

164

Walter jingled his key chain out of his pocket, then began the agonizing process of flipping through them for the right one.

Snowflakes dampened the shoulders of their coats. Michael shivered.

Walter worked to feed the key in the hole; perhaps he'd lost track of his scotches somewhere along the way.

Elizabeth let out a yelp of happiness as Walter freed up the door and reset the alarm.

"I want a safe deposit box," she announced.

"You mean you want to get in your safe deposit box?" Walter asked.

"No—well, I want that, too. But I need a new one. In Michael's name. It's my Christmas gift."

"A safe deposit box?" Walter wheezed a laugh. "Not exactly the stuff of great Christmas fantasies."

"Maybe not, but what I'm going to put in it will be."

She reached into her pocketbook, taking out the key she had somehow not returned to her rolltop desk in the living room. Had she been foolish carrying it along with the change in her billfold, where it could so easily get lost or stolen? Or had she simply wanted to be ready for the moment when her idea would find her?

Walter got her second deposit box key. Handed it over. Began the paperwork for a box for Michael, who remained rooted inside the entrance looking completely confused.

Elizabeth raced past the vault, into the safe deposit box room. Her hands shook so much she could hardly get both keys in. She turned the locks, pulled her box out, and raced to the viewing table.

She found it quickly. The green diamond.

But before Elizabeth could pick it up, another hand reached into her safe deposit box.

"No one else is supposed to be in here," Elizabeth said foolishly. As though she'd been interrupted by a stranger. No one else was in the bank, not at this hour, not on Christmas Eve.

Elizabeth followed the hand—a woman's, with painted red nails and knuckles grown large with age—as it picked up the ring.

And there she was. The woman from Elizabeth's childhood kitchen. Her violet eyes moved from the green diamond to Elizabeth's face.

"You've made an old woman quite happy," she said.

"Old woman," Elizabeth repeated. "The papers were wrong. Your story didn't end in '32, did it? Here you are. I didn't dream you up. I couldn't have. You gave me something real. Something I could hold in my hands."

"Is that what makes something real?" the woman asked. "Someone else telling you that they see the same thing? Is that what makes something valuable? Finding someone else who agrees with you about an item's worth?"

The woman had never spoken to Elizabeth before. Not since that winter day before Christmas so long ago. When Elizabeth had been a child in her mother's handed-down dress, a garment worn out by chores that had not been her own.

"I'm sure Tom didn't need a soul to tell him they'd looked out their front window on Christmas Eve and seen him and his father having a catch, out in the snow, under the moonlight," the woman said. "I'm sure that it was real to *him*."

"How do you know about Tom?" Elizabeth asked.

But the woman didn't respond. Not directly. Without mentioning Tom's name, she said, "Something can always be of value to you that seems worthless to the rest of the world."

When Elizabeth reached out to touch her, the woman's entire image rippled outward, like the surface of a lake hit with a skipping stone. And then she was gone. The green diamond ring clinked on the viewing table.

Elizabeth glanced about the room, hoping to see her in some corner. Funny—when the woman had been standing in front of her, she'd looked so lifelike. Now, mere seconds after disappearing, she seemed to Elizabeth like something she had imagined, nothing more. Some fanciful but hazy daydream. Maybe, she thought, there in the safe deposit area, surrounded by boxes crammed with heirlooms and deeds that had followed the branches of a family tree, that was simply the nature of memories. Maybe memories traveled in our heads like ghosts, always there, waiting to be seen out the corner of our eyes. Not for public viewing.

She closed her box, returned it to its proper slot, and hurried out to where Walter, Michael, and Tom were all waiting.

"Here," she said, as the door fell shut behind her with an official-sounding *thunk*.

"This goes in his box." She stretched her hand out, holding the ring.

"Elizabeth," Walter breathed. "Are you sure?"

"I am."

"But your niece."

"My estate will go to her family. She'll be fine. She'll have everything she needs. But this ring is a different story. Its history is part of its value, too."

Turning to Michael, she said, "Finish school. Start a business. Market your amps. That music you help share—it's something. It's not just the people who make the clothes or make the music who are important. It's people like you that make sure the music gets heard. Maybe even people like me, who can get the clothes on the right women. We can market happiness, Michael. That's what it's all about. I feel it with absolute certainty. You can make people happy. What you're doing is important. It's not a frivolous thing."

"But you don't know me. I even tried to rob you."

Elizabeth ignored him. "The most valuable part of this is the story that goes with it. I used to feel like I gave something away every time I told the story, and so for the most part, I didn't tell it. But that's wrong. The value *is* in the story, but the value grows with the telling. It has to be shared."

"What story?" Michael asked.

"Walter can tell it to you. He knows it."

Michael glanced up at Walter, bewildered.

"What I want in return," Elizabeth said. "My one condition—" She waited for him to look at her again before she continued, "—is that you promise to do something for someone else. Take a chance on someone. That's the history of this ring and its future. And the person you take a chance on has to be someone you don't know. The ultimate gamble. Once your dream is realized, promise that you'll pass the ring's gift on. The right person and the right time will present itself to you."

He nodded limply, not sure exactly what he'd agreed to.

Elizabeth started for the door. "Oh, and Michael—" she called.

"Yes?"

"I don't want to see you in my store every time I look up. Okay? I don't want you ever to feel you're beholden to me. You're not. I want your face turned forward, toward tomorrow and the tomorrow after. See what I mean?"

"I think so," he said.

Elizabeth smiled. "You will. It will get clearer as time goes by."

"Son, this ring has quite the story," Walter started to tell Michael, as Elizabeth raced for the door. Giggling, like a girl.

Outside, Tom raced to catch up with Elizabeth. "That wasn't exactly what I had in mind," he told her.

"It's right. This is the best feeling I've ever had on any Christmas Eve. Better even than the year I got that ring. I think that's what she gave me. More than anything. *This* year—getting a chance to do this unexpected thing—that was the true gift. Wasn't it? It's such a wonderful feeling. I hope she felt like this, the year she gave me that ring."

Tom put his hands on her waist and drew her close. There they were, as the snow swirled, the street empty of everything but Christmas Eve's soft yellow glow.

"This is like standing in a Christmas card," she told him.

He offered a faint smile.

"You do like Christmas cards again, don't you?" she murmured.

He drew her still closer. The night air should have been cold. It should have tingled against Elizabeth's skin. But the world felt warm as she raised her chin and closed her eyes. Tom smelled like Ruby's Place—like pine and chocolate and marshmallows. And he smelled like old letters. Like cedar boxes. Like something special that was meant to be preserved. Like something that she wanted to always have. She leaned forward; when her lips found his, they also found a snowflake right there on his mouth.

And, finally, fifty-year-old Elizabeth found love.

He pulled away enough to tell her, "You're the rarest gem of all, Lizzie."

As they embraced again, arms around each other, cheek pressed to cheek, a shadowy figure joined them on the sidewalk. One with violet eyes and a black cloak. Waving goodbye.

It could have been a moment's fancy. A trick of light. Elizabeth's eyes could have been watering enough to see anything she wanted.

She didn't need to ask Tom if he saw her.

Because if Elizabeth was certain of anything, it was that there really was magic in this particular Christmas Eve.

20.

Ruby burst through the bright green door on the front of her supper club and plopped down on her bench, an old fashioned in her hand.

Someone immediately sat beside her. She expected it to be Walter, back from whatever that trip with Elizabeth had been. But when she turned, she found a police officer.

"Taking five?" she asked. "Kind of a rotten night to be on foot patrol."

"I don't mind it," he admitted. "Christmas Eve is different."

Ruby nodded knowingly. "You need a coat—you know you do—but on Christmas Eve, the night feels warm, somehow."

He smiled. "That's it exactly."

A roar bled through the bricks from inside her bar.

"Rowdy tonight," he observed.

"Always is on Christmas Eve."

"You taking a breather of your own?" he asked.

"I miss Ida. She helped me get this place open. Such a character. And did that old gal have the recipes. Those are her marshmallows, you know. The ones I serve inside? The homemade ones everybody always talks up? She could make a pile of grass taste like steak."

"Ida," he repeated.

"The way you said her name makes me think you knew her."

"I heard tales from some old-timers on the force."

"Did you, now?"

The streetlights sparkled against her cocktail glass as she held it toward the officer. "Here. Have a sip."

"I'm on duty."

"I don't usually drink at all on Christmas Eve," Ruby said. "It's such a busy night. But I can't get Ida out of my mind."

"Easy to miss someone on Christmas."

"I wanted to honor Ida this year, and it all just seems so shallow," Ruby admitted. "It's crazy, really. I've got so much—my best friend Elizabeth and her niece and everyone here tonight. But losing her really rattled me. It's so hard to lose somebody. I just keep thinking if only I could see her one more time. Tell her everything that's been on my mind, everything I've realized since she passed.

"You know," Ruby went on, "I keep thinking how I can't be the only person who feels that way. How great it would be if we could always have this place for special friends or families or lovers to meet up. If memories— those ghosts of Christmases past—could come back to life. Even for a single night. Can you imagine? What better night than Christmas? I wish Ida could stop by here, and let me know how she is, like always. What I wouldn't give to see her one more time. What I wouldn't give to show her how this place has grown, even in the short handful of months since I last saw her. I wish—"

"Ah, a wish."

"Yes. I wish that this place could continue on forever. That we'd always be able to celebrate here, that there was no such thing as a long-lost loved one. That we'd never have to let go of nights like this."

When the officer didn't answer, she began to feel a little foolish. Some gray-haired old woman and her silly imaginings. She squeaked, "Well, you know what I mean. Don't you?"

She turned, but the bench was empty. Ruby's only company was a cardinal hopping down the sidewalk.

"Huh," Ruby said, taking a sip of her drink. The liquor warmed her chest as she crossed her legs and slumped down, finding the exact spot she'd worn comfortable on the bench.

"Hey," she said to the cardinal, "you didn't happen to catch the name printed on that officer's uniform, did you? Could've sworn it said Barister. That's Elizabeth's new guy's last name. Does Tom have someone else on the force? A brother, you think? Maybe even a younger brother? Looked awfully similar."

The cardinal cocked his head to the side.

"Probably not," Ruby said. She raised the glass to her lips again. "So similar, though. Like father and son."

The cardinal hopped a few steps closer.

"Cardinals appear when angels are near," Ruby recited, raising her glass to him.

21.

December, 2022

A man walked along the square in Sullivan. A stranger, or so it seemed to the shoppers and the store owners, none of which knew his name. He was older, with white hair and a full white beard. In a topcoat and a pair of leather boots that were clearly expensive. Most wondered what he was doing there, especially when he kept stopping, reading aloud from the signs that hung above store entrances. When he mumbled to himself, "I thought the old electronics shop used to be right around here."

It had, of course, though Weber's Electronics had been out of business by then for quite some time.

"Would have thought one of Roy's kids would

take over," the stranger muttered, which really got a couple's attention.

How could he have known about Roy?

The stranger passed the It Ain't Over Yet flea market and The Page Turner bookstore. He paused on the sidewalk, staring at a square that had been inscribed when the cement was still fresh: *Rob & Geena 4Ever 1987.*

"Young love," said the mail carrier, following the stranger's gaze.

"Must have been done right at the beginning of their story," the stranger said. "Wonder where their beginning led."

The mail carrier smiled; he knew exactly where it had gone. Knew the story in full. Would have been happy to tell it, never mind that he didn't know this man. That was how stories were in Sullivan. Gossip, some called it. Not this particular mail carrier, though. It was part of the story of Sullivan. It was *their* story, all of them.

But the stranger cut him off by saying, "I have a beginning to give myself. If only I could figure out who to give it to."

He glanced up at Ruby's bright green door. And he pushed through it, stepping inside.

The woman at the bar surprised him, though she shouldn't have. No way could Ruby still be mixing up her hot chocolates and serving her homemade marshmallows. This woman was no Ruby—no ballerina grace. She was middle-aged and graying, with one of those friendly faces that you couldn't help wanting to get closer to.

She smiled, but he thought it was a little guarded. Or maybe the stares from outside had made him interpret it that way. Really, he'd anticipated that response. No one in Sullivan could have recognized him, not with that white hair of his and that slightly arthritic gait. He had acquired a bad knee from an accident in his thirties. But by then, he was long gone from Sullivan.

The woman behind the bar tried to turn her attention to stacking glasses, but she kept her eyes on him like she figured he was looking the place over. He was, too—not like he was thinking of robbing it, though. More like someone who was thinking about making it his own.

She'd worked hard on the place. And she didn't like the way this guy was looking around at it. She didn't like that at all.

Ruby's was mostly empty that time of the after-noon. The woman at the bar had no one to block her view as he wandered right over to the piano, sat on the bench, and leaned down to touch something on the floor.

She slipped out from behind the ornate, carved antique bar. Wiping her hands on a white towel, she walked to the piano. "Get you something?" she asked.

He looked right at her. But he was uninterested in a drink.

"Don't remember seeing you around," she pressed.

"I grew up here."

"Yeah? Me, too. I'm Angela." She offered a hand to shake, but he was uninterested in that, too.

He was more interested in the floor.

"Oh, that," Angela said, realizing he was looking at the amp. "It's really old. Evie—the piano player that was here when Ruby was—she used to mic her piano on Christmas Eve."

"Does it still work?"

"It does. It was in with some old stuff of Ruby's in the back."

"I can't believe it. Still here."

"It almost wasn't. Ruby's Place closed down. I bought it and reopened a few years ago."

"You had to reopen Ruby's?" he asked.

"It had fallen on some bad times."

"Had it?"

Angela shrugged. "Time wreaks havoc on everything."

"Why you?"

Angela offered the slightest hint of a grin. "That's a bit of a story. Let's just say I took after my aunt. Started a business late in life."

"Ruby was your aunt?"

"No—Elizabeth Rossi. She used to own—"

"A dress store," he finished.

"You really are from Sullivan."

He nodded, smiling. "She gave me something, your Aunt Elizabeth. A Christmas present. Long ago."

"A ring, maybe?"

He was startled by this. Then he brightened. "It's rightfully yours!" Relief washed over his face.

But Angela was already shaking her head. "Elizabeth warned me about this. She said you might try to give it back. She made me promise not to take it, *Michael.*" She added his name to prove Elizabeth really had shared the story.

"It's junk, you know," he said.

"The ring?"

"Yeah. Funniest thing. When she gave it to me, she acted like it was really something valuable. Took out a safe deposit box for it in my name. Had Walter tell me this entire story about it—about it being a gift from a stranger during the Depression."

Angela didn't say anything. That look on her face, though—it wasn't unlike the look the mail carrier had worn, the one that said he knew the whole story of the Rob and Geena in the sidewalk square.

"I really needed something valuable," Michael went on. "I needed that ring to be something. Your aunt didn't know it, but my dad was really sick. He died right after the new year. I knew it was going to happen that Christmas. Deep down, I mean. But that didn't keep me from holding on to hope."

He shook his head at himself, remembering. "I used to volunteer at this daycare for old folks. I had this fantasy about Dad becoming an old man. Me having to visit him in one of those places. She caught me there once, but I never told her why I went there. We didn't have a lot of money. Rented our house and—when he was gone—I thought I could cash that ring in. I was so ready. A real break, like you only read about. Her taking a chance on me. Someone she barely even knew."

"And then you took it somewhere to sell it, and found out," Angela said.

"Yeah, the appraiser laughed at me. Said it was costume jewelry."

"Must have been a shock."

"Oh, the appraiser said there was still a market for it. Said costume collectors liked certain names. The woman who made the ring your aunt gave me—her pieces have always been fairly rare, so the guy told me what I had was worth three or four hundred."

"Three or four…hundred. Not exactly what a young man who suddenly has no father—who's thinking of supporting himself and his mother, maybe even starting his own business—wants to hear," Angela said.

"Right. I could hardly believe it. I figured your aunt had stuff in her jewelry box at home worth more. She had to have been aware. Walter at the bank had to have been aware. At first, I felt so duped. But then it hit me: *Walter at the bank had to know.* But he let her use that thing as collateral so she could open her shop? Not good practice, obviously. Not something that would ever take place at a bank in any other town. But what trust that took. What belief. What a chance he took on her."

He sat still on the bench. Almost like the statues outside the Sullivan Public Library.

"And that *story* of hers," Michael went on. "The one she told Walter, that Walter told me. About Christmas and a back-door knock. Did she make it up? I mean, the ring had to come from somewhere. Was there ever really a woman? One that she thought she saw again later on? Did the visit to the jeweler really happen? Did he really tell her and her mother that ring was valuable? Why? Did he make a mistake? *Did* he tell Elizabeth and her mother that it was costume? Or could he not bear to tell them the truth, not then, not in the midst of such horrible times? Did he just want to give them the gift of hope, in such short supply then? What really happened that winter day?"

"Hope was probably in short supply for you, too, without your dad around," Angela said.

"The only sense I could make of it was that she wanted to give me the gift of hope. That she was telling *me* to believe. To believe in myself."

Michael raised his head. "A little corny?"

"It's not corny if it kept you moving," Angela said.

"It kept me *seeing*," Michael corrected. "People are always taking chances on each other. We don't notice. We see the grand gestures. But in small ways, smaller gestures, people do. They take chances. They use your amp at a special event. They drop your name to someone who can open a door. They give you ten dollars when they only have twelve. She made me see the world differently. It was the way I saw the world that made me not want to quit, even when times got rocky. It made me believe in goodness. In...magic. What I wouldn't give to see her now, tell her thank you."

"The way you talk about her—it's so different than the memories I had of her when I was a kid," Angela admitted. "When I was a kid, I thought of Aunt Elizabeth as...standoffish, almost. I thought she was kind, of course—one of the kindest people I knew. But a little severe. Not exactly the motherly sort."

"Really?" Michael asked. "I didn't see her that way at all."

"You have to admit she wasn't exactly huggy. I remember, I used to greet her by kind of throwing myself at her, almost like she couldn't refuse my embrace."

"I never noticed. Maybe I never expected her to be that way. Maybe, as her niece, you did."

"Sometimes," Angela said, "I think I just didn't see. Not back then. You know, she met someone when she was older. The love of her life. And I had no idea. He was right here, under my nose, and I didn't see it. How could I miss that?"

"Each human being is such a mystery," Michael muttered. "So many times, I've thought what Elizabeth wanted me to think about is what is real."

"Real," Angela repeated. And, "Magic." She stared at him a long time. Like she was trying to make some sort of decision. "I might have a story for you."

"About Elizabeth?"

Angela pointed up toward the bar. "Why don't I make you something?"

He glanced down at the amp again. "An idea would be good."

"Sorry?"

"It's why I came back to Sullivan. I decided this is the year I make good on that promise to your aunt. Time to figure out who gets that ring next. I don't have a clue right now, though."

"You've come to the perfect spot," Angela said. "Magical things happen in Ruby's Place. Around Christmas."

"That's when Elizabeth gave me her ring. On Christmas Eve."

"I know." Angela tossed her head again, in the direction of the bar. "Come on. We'll see if we can begin to figure something out. In the meantime, I happen to have in my possession the very best of all of Ruby's recipes."

Figures in the shadows had overheard Michael's

story. They watched as the pair walked toward the bar.

In two weeks, it would be Christmas.

And Christmas had plenty of plans of its own.

Come Back to Ruby's

What kind of story did Angela tell Michael about Ruby's Place? Find out in the original Ruby's Place Christmas Collection, available now:

Christmas at Ruby's

I Remember You

Sentimental Journey

The Gift That Is Ruby's Place

Ruby's Story,

the prequel to Rare Gems and the story of how Ruby came to own the magical supper club, is also available:

Holly Schindler

Holly Schindler is an author of books for readers of all ages. Her books have received starred reviews in PW and Booklist, and won both the silver medal in Foreword IN-DIES Book of the Year and the gold medal in the IPPY Awards. She is currently drinking too much coffee while writing her next book.

Check out her other titles, get in touch, or subscribe to her newsletter(s) at:

HollySchindler.com

www.ingramcontent.com/pod-product-compliance
Lightning Source LLC
Chambersburg PA
CBHW030631190726
48286CB00008B/2483